T1-BLH-759

STONE ARCH BOOKS
a capstone imprint

STONE ARCH BOOKS™

Published in 2012
A Capstone Imprint
1710 Roe Crest Drive
North Mankato, MN 56003
www.capstonepub.com

Originally published by DC Comics in the U.S. in
single magazine form as Tiny Titans #1.
Copyright © 2012 DC Comics. All Rights Reserved.

DC Comics
1700 Broadway, New York, NY 10019
A Warner Bros. Entertainment Company

No part of this publication may be reproduced in whole or in
part, or stored in a retrieval system, or transmitted in any
form or by any means, electronic, mechanical, photocopying,
recording, or otherwise, without written permission.

Cataloging-in-Publication Data is available at the Library of
Congress website:
ISBN: 978-1-4342-4528-1 (library binding)

Summary: Meet the new staff of Sidekick City Elementary!
Plus, see your favorite Titans in their
cutest possible forms!

STONE ARCH BOOKS

Ashley C. Andersen Zantop *Publisher*
Michael Dahl *Editorial Director*
Donald Lemke & Alison Deering *Editors*
Heather Kindseth *Creative Director*
Hilary Wacholz *Designer*
Kathy McColley *Production Specialist*

DC COMICS

Jann Jones *Original U.S. Editor*
Stephanie Buscema *U.S. Assistant Editor*
Nick J. Napolitano *Letterer*

Printed in the United States of America
in North Mankato, Minnesota.
032015 008835R

Sidekick City Elementary
33305234672156
0jgn   05/11/16

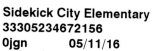

tiny titans

Sidekick City Elementary

By Eisner Winners
Art Baltazar & Franco

tiny titans

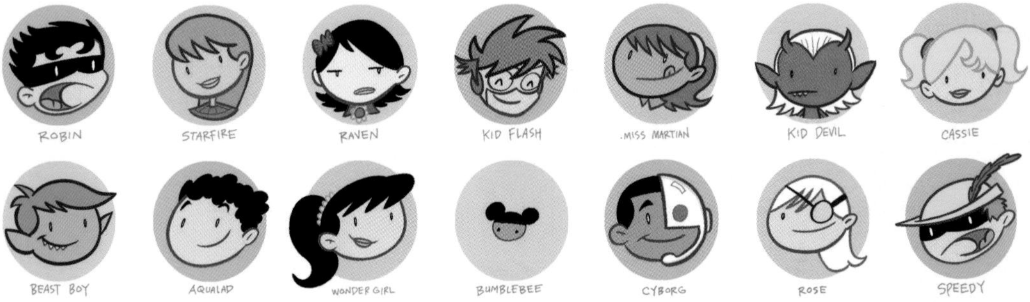
ROBIN
STARFIRE
RAVEN
KID FLASH
MISS MARTIAN
KID DEVIL
CASSIE
BEAST BOY
AQUALAD
WONDER GIRL
BUMBLEBEE
CYBORG
ROSE
SPEEDY

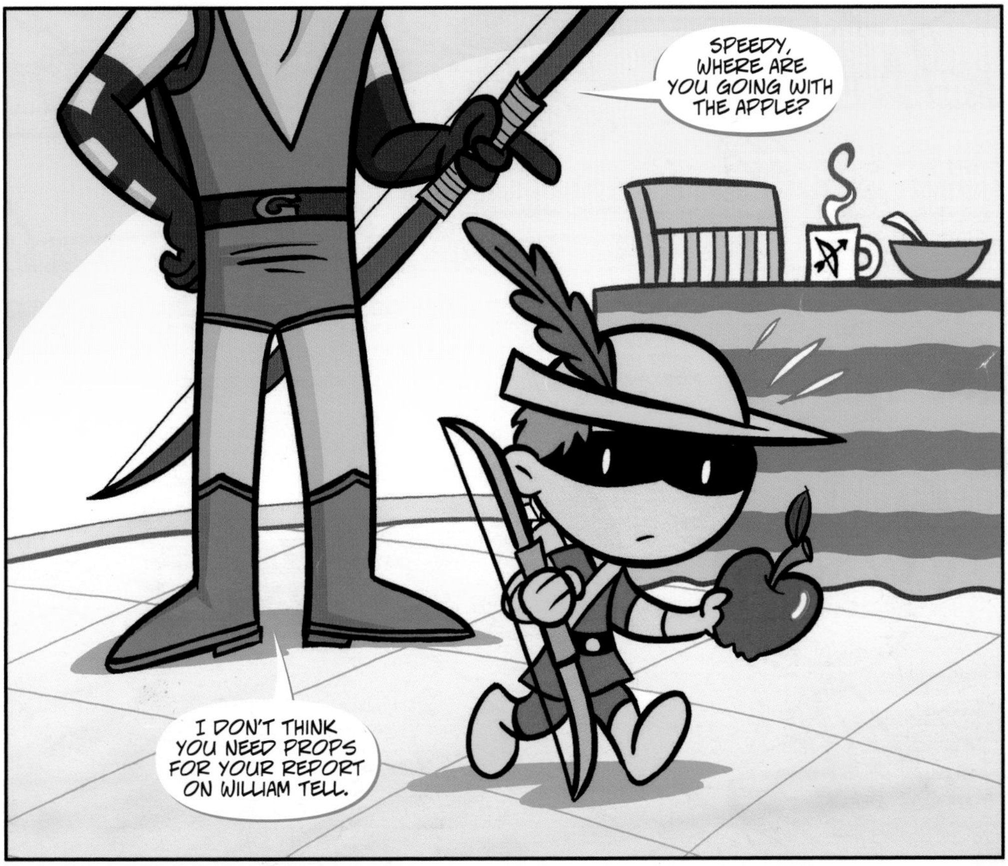
SPEEDY, WHERE ARE YOU GOING WITH THE APPLE?
I DON'T THINK YOU NEED PROPS FOR YOUR REPORT ON WILLIAM TELL.

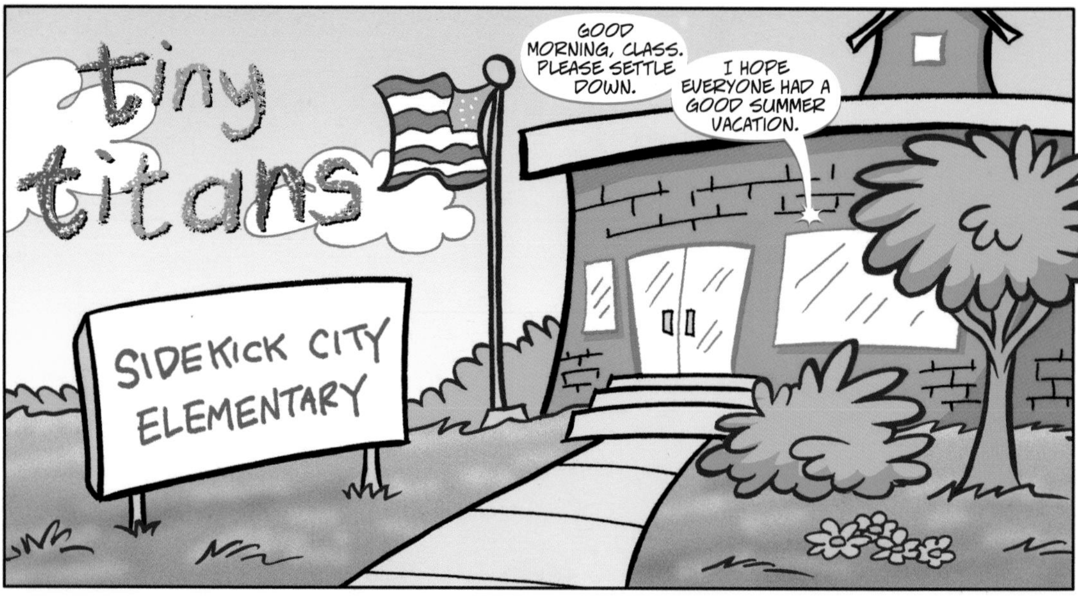
tiny titans
GOOD MORNING, CLASS. PLEASE SETTLE DOWN.
I HOPE EVERYONE HAD A GOOD SUMMER VACATION.
SIDEKICK CITY ELEMENTARY

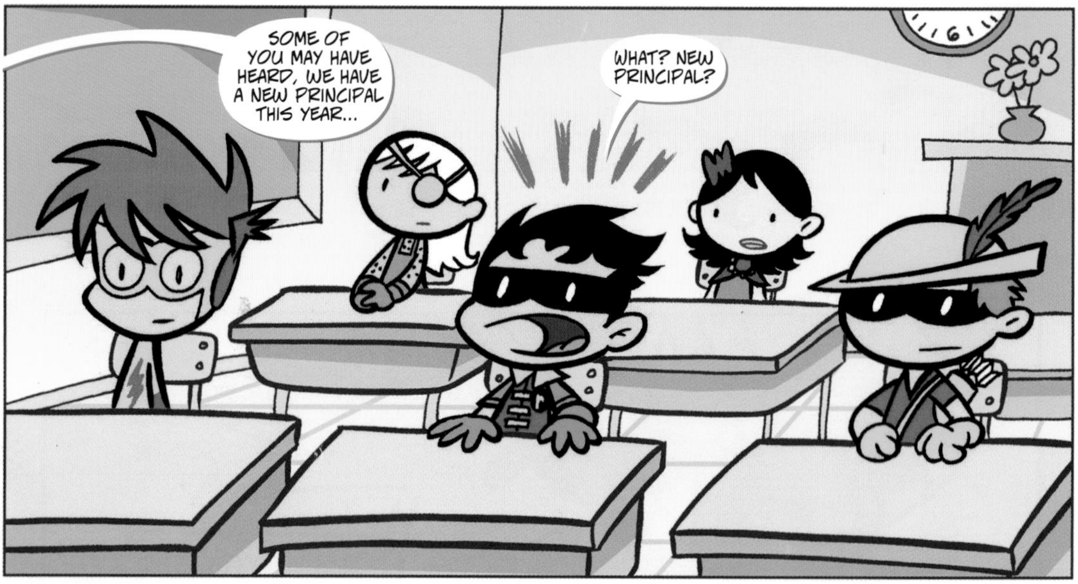
SOME OF YOU MAY HAVE HEARD, WE HAVE A NEW PRINCIPAL THIS YEAR...
WHAT? NEW PRINCIPAL?

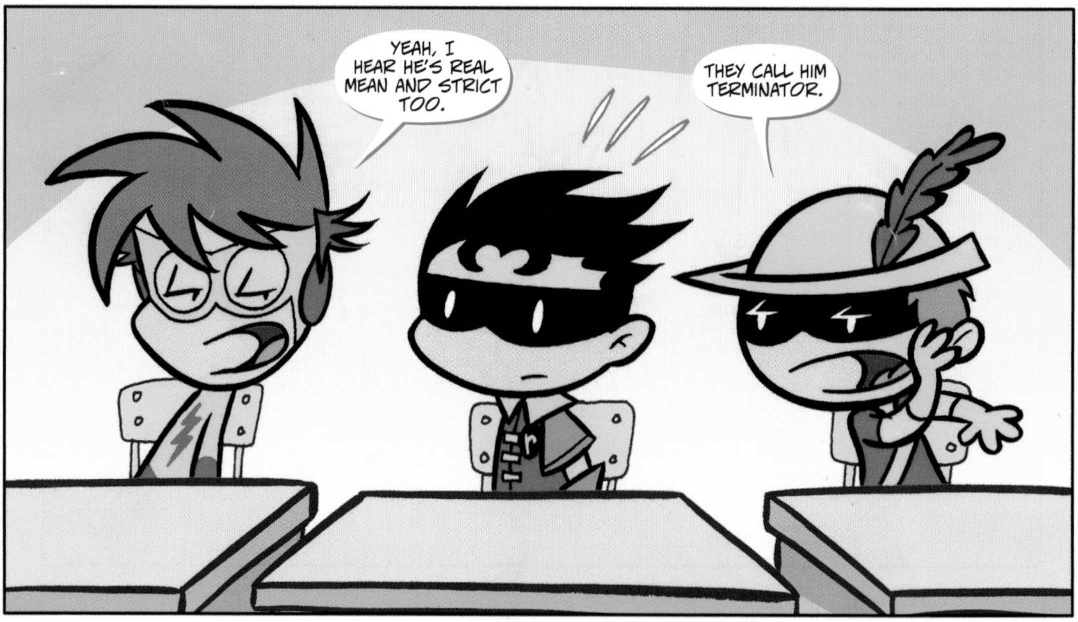
YEAH, I HEAR HE'S REAL MEAN AND STRICT TOO.
THEY CALL HIM TERMINATOR.

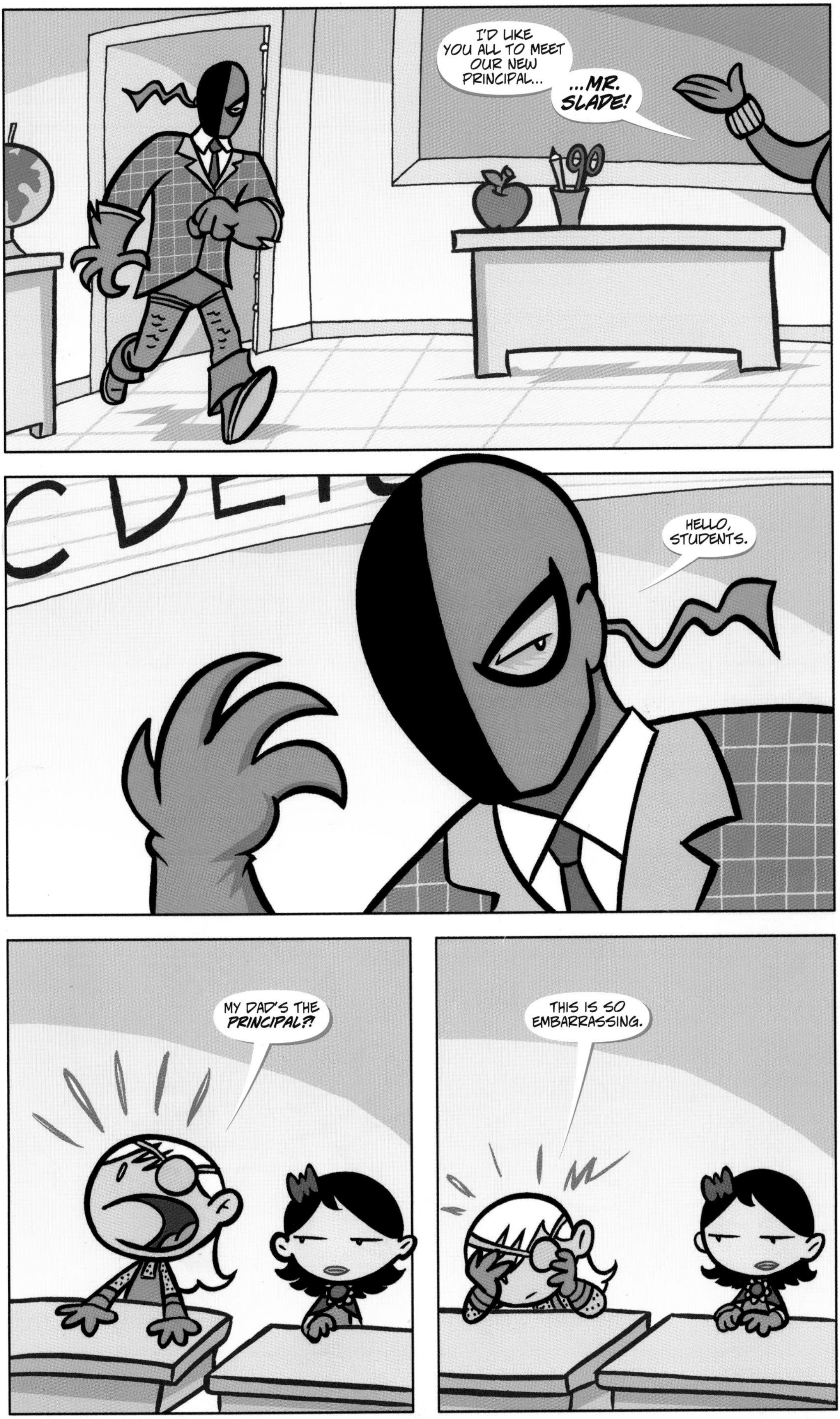
I'D LIKE YOU ALL TO MEET OUR NEW PRINCIPAL...
...MR. SLADE!
HELLO, STUDENTS.
MY DAD'S THE PRINCIPAL?!
THIS IS SO EMBARRASSING.

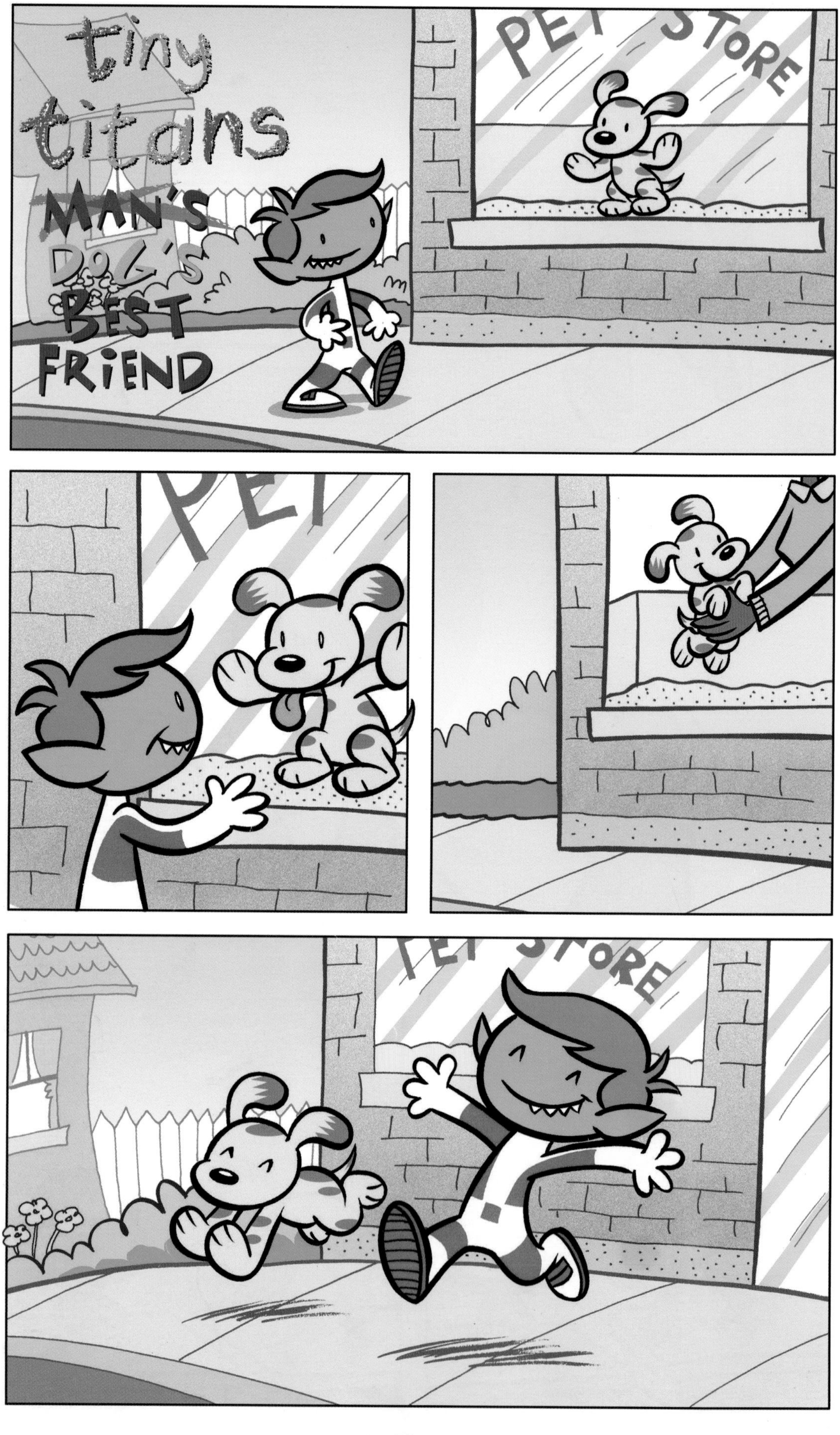
tiny titans
MAN'S
DOG'S
BEST
FRIEND
PET STORE

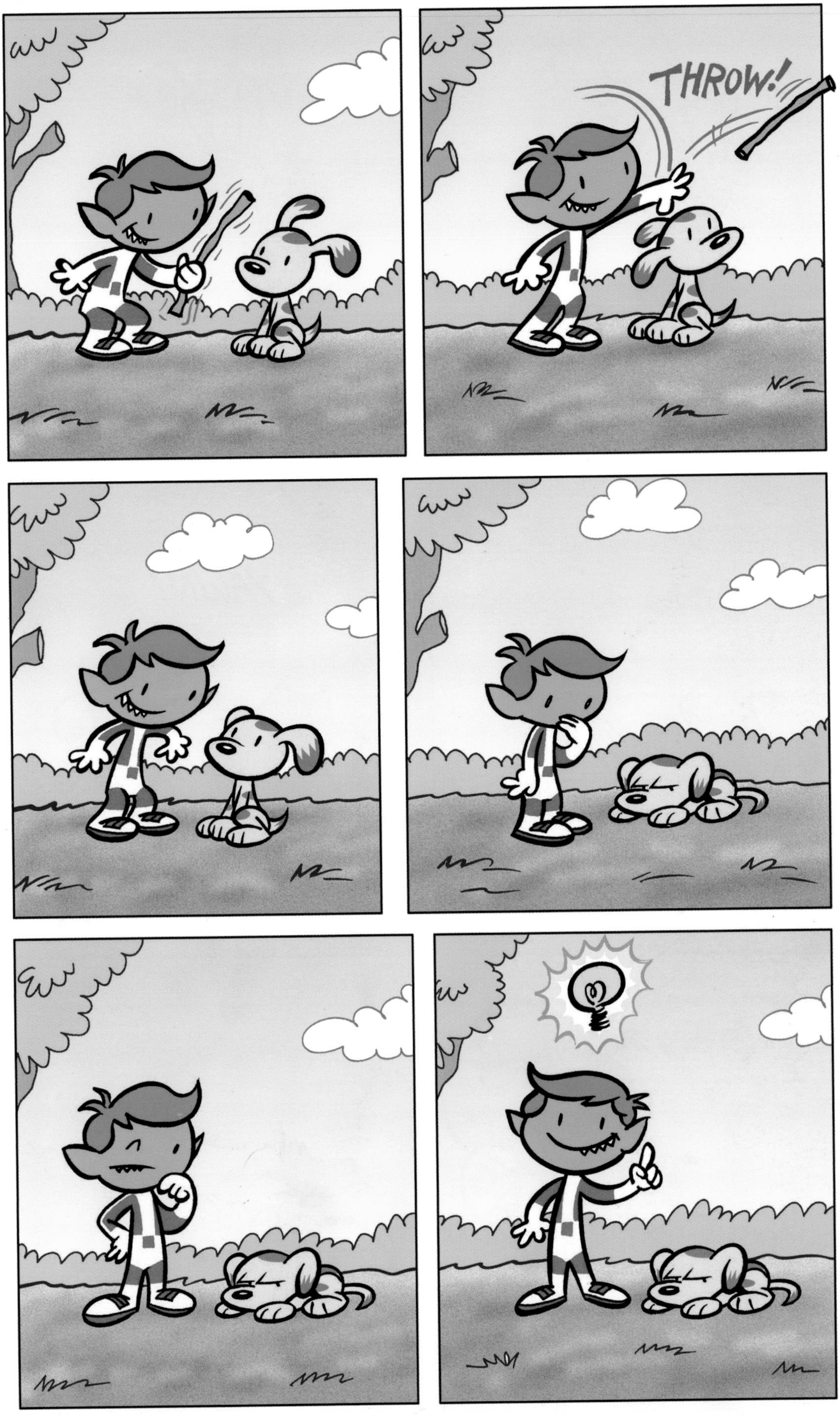
THROW!

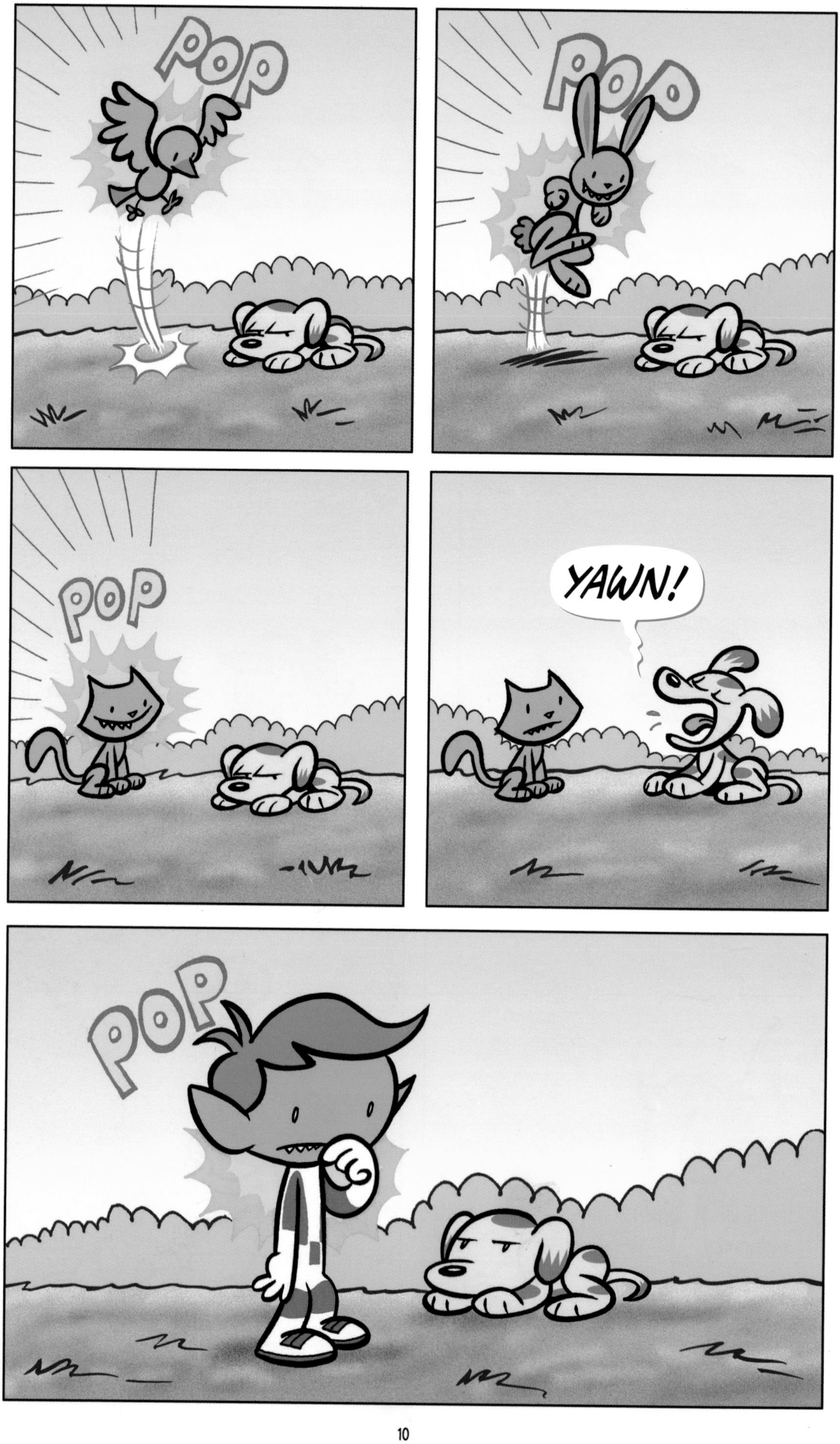
POP
POP
POP
YAWN!
POP

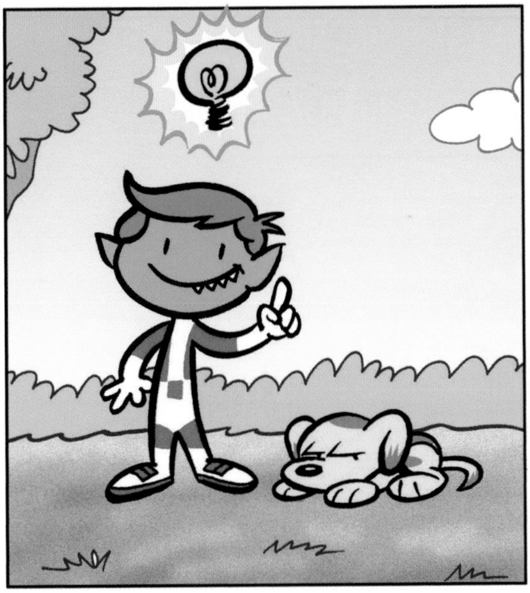

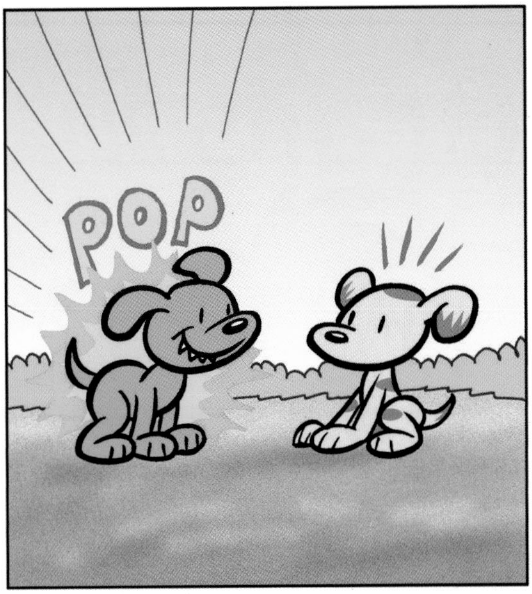
POP

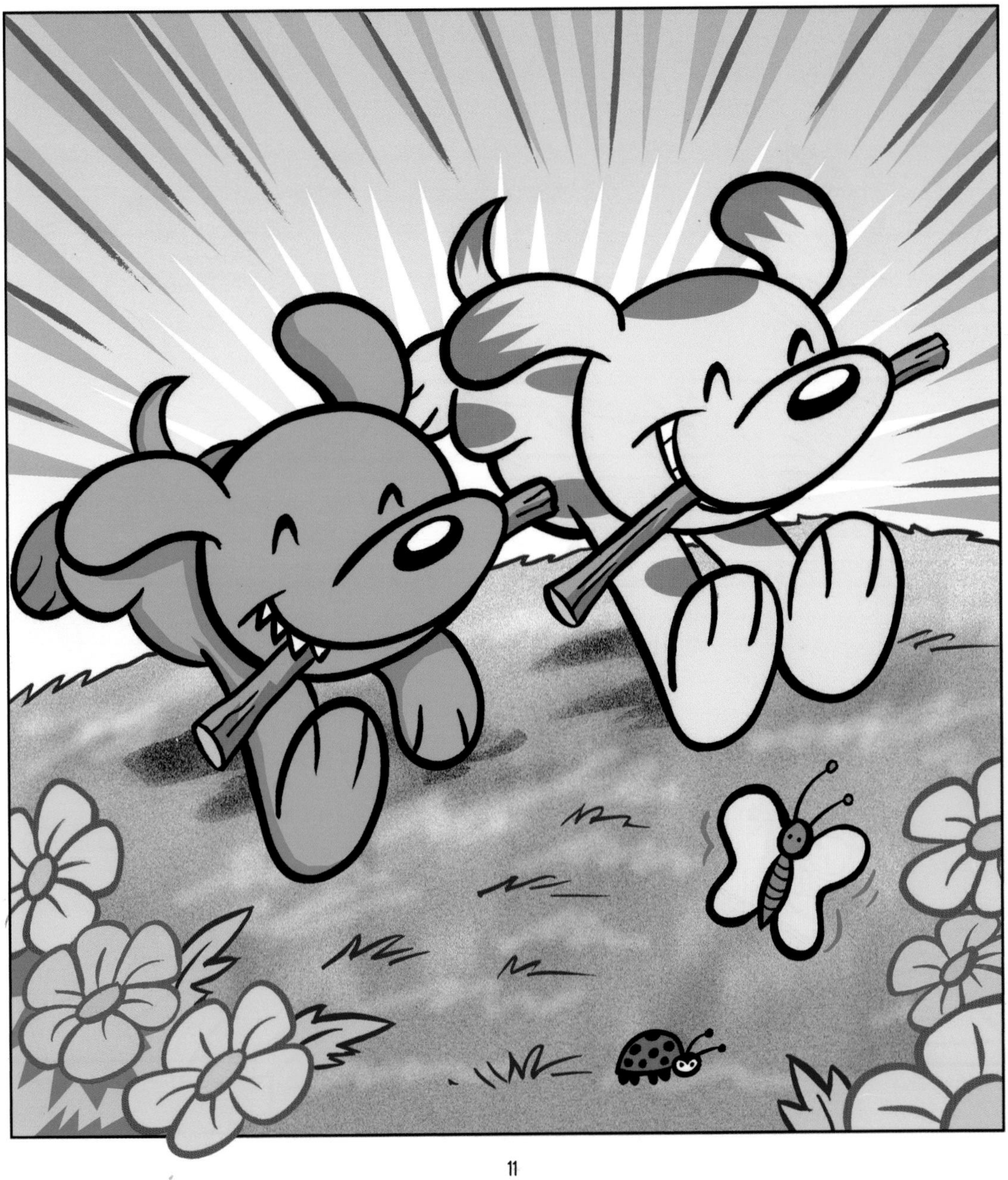

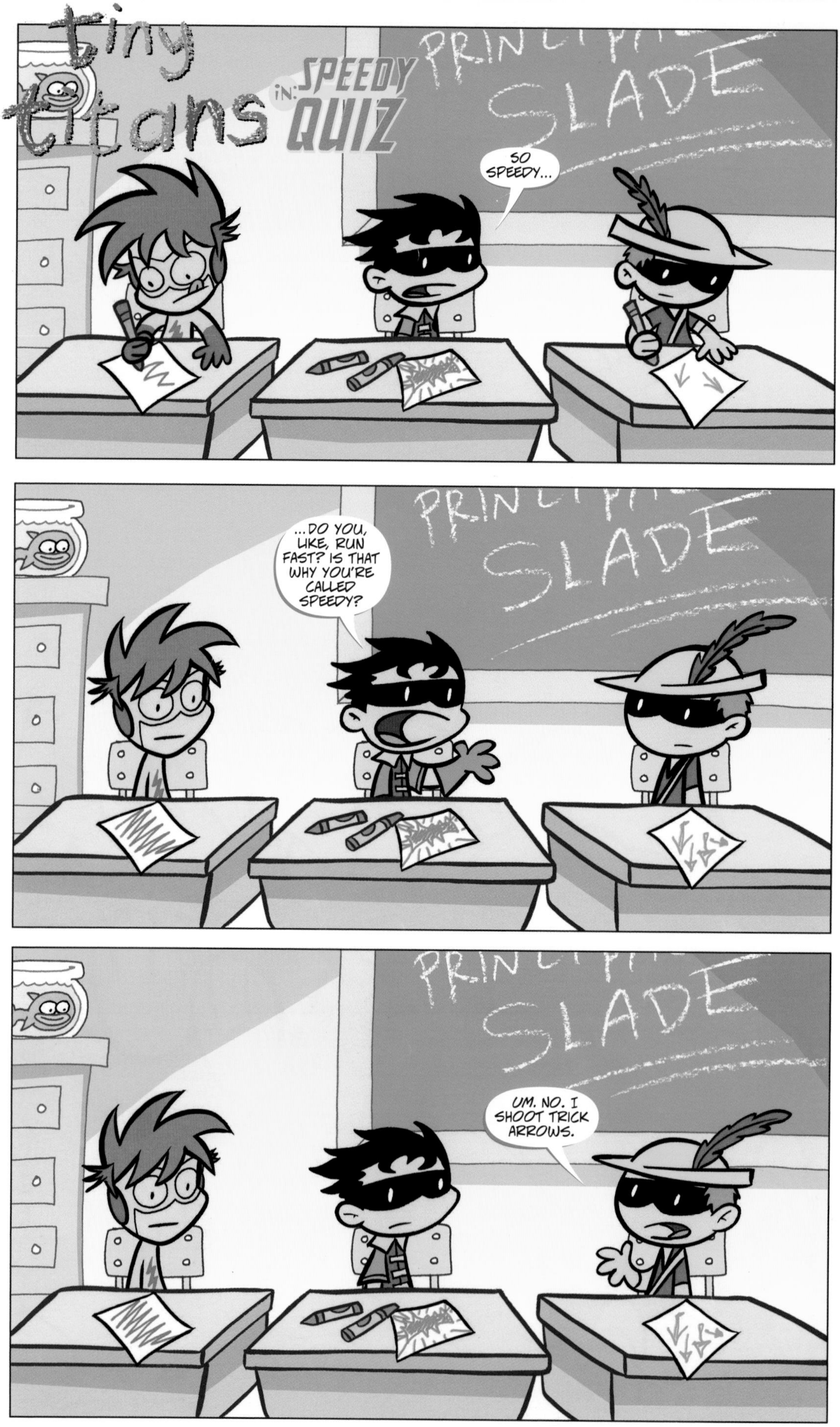
tiny titans
in: SPEEDY QUIZ
PRINCIPAL
SLADE
SO SPEEDY...
...DO YOU, LIKE, RUN FAST? IS THAT WHY YOU'RE CALLED SPEEDY?
UM. NO. I SHOOT TRICK ARROWS.

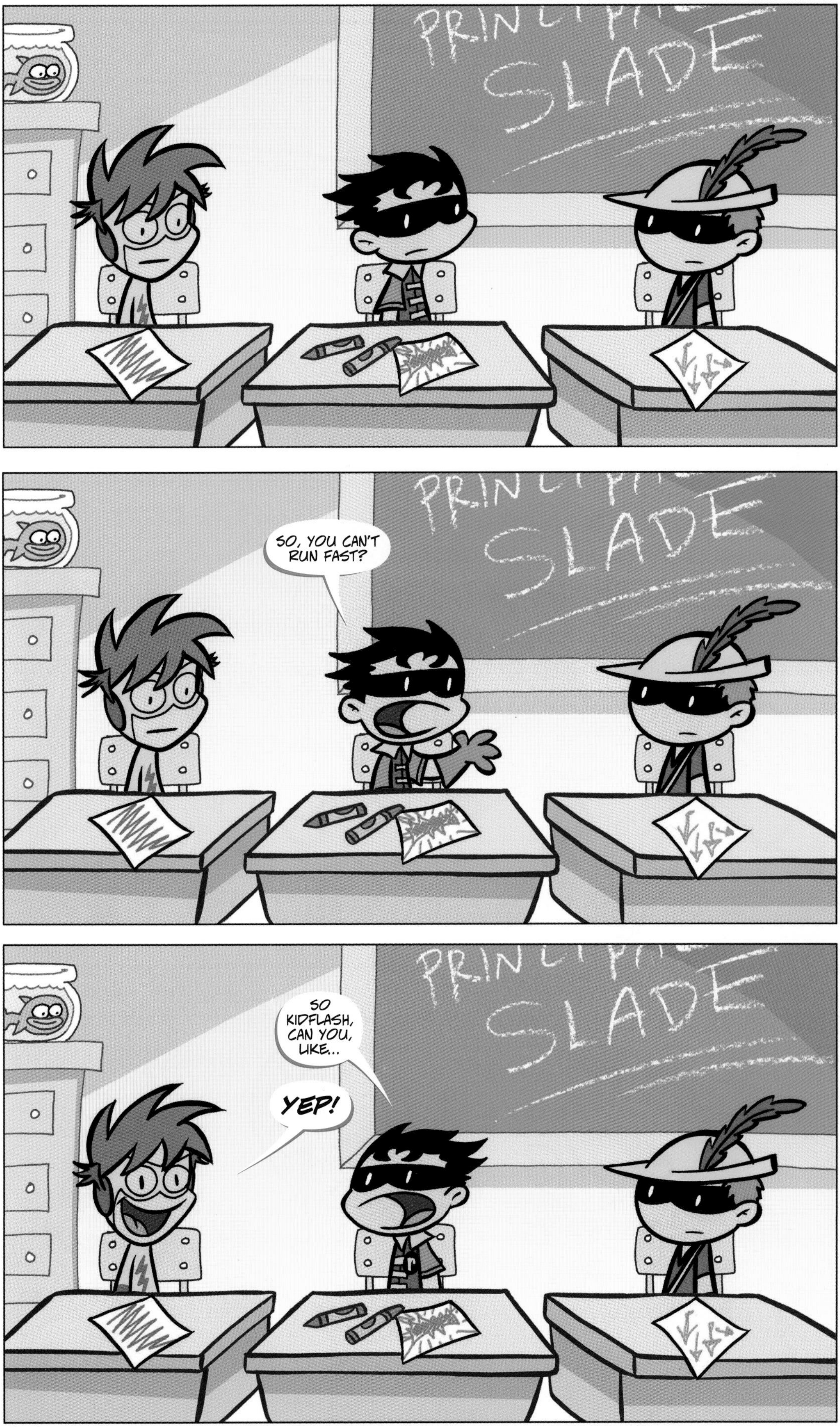
PRIN CI PA
SLADE
SO, YOU CAN'T RUN FAST?
SO KIDFLASH, CAN YOU, LIKE...
YEP!

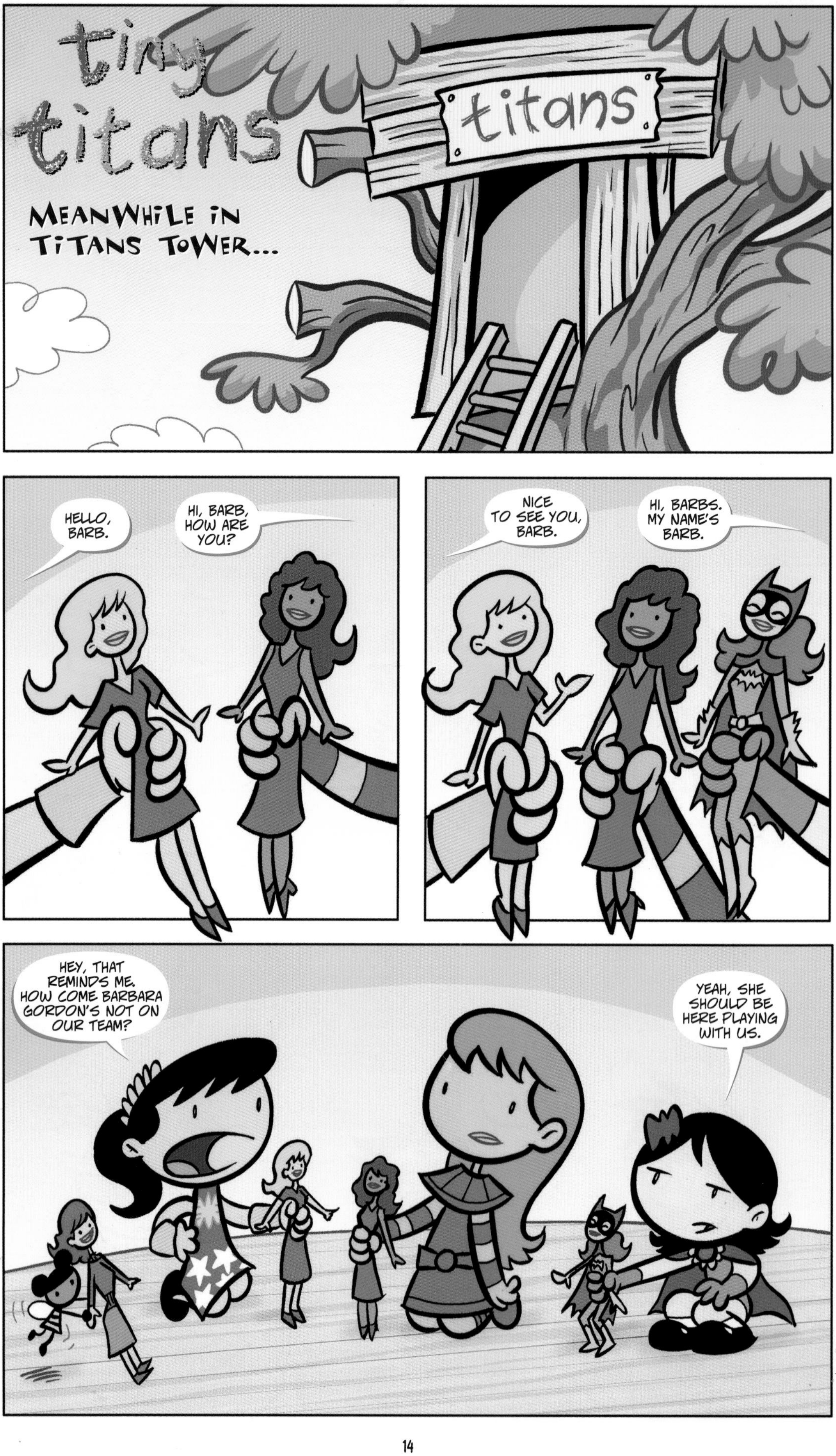

tiny titans
titans
MEANWHILE IN TITANS TOWER...
HELLO, BARB.
HI, BARB, HOW ARE YOU?
NICE TO SEE YOU, BARB.
HI, BARBS. MY NAME'S BARB.
HEY, THAT REMINDS ME. HOW COME BARBARA GORDON'S NOT ON OUR TEAM?
YEAH, SHE SHOULD BE HERE PLAYING WITH US.

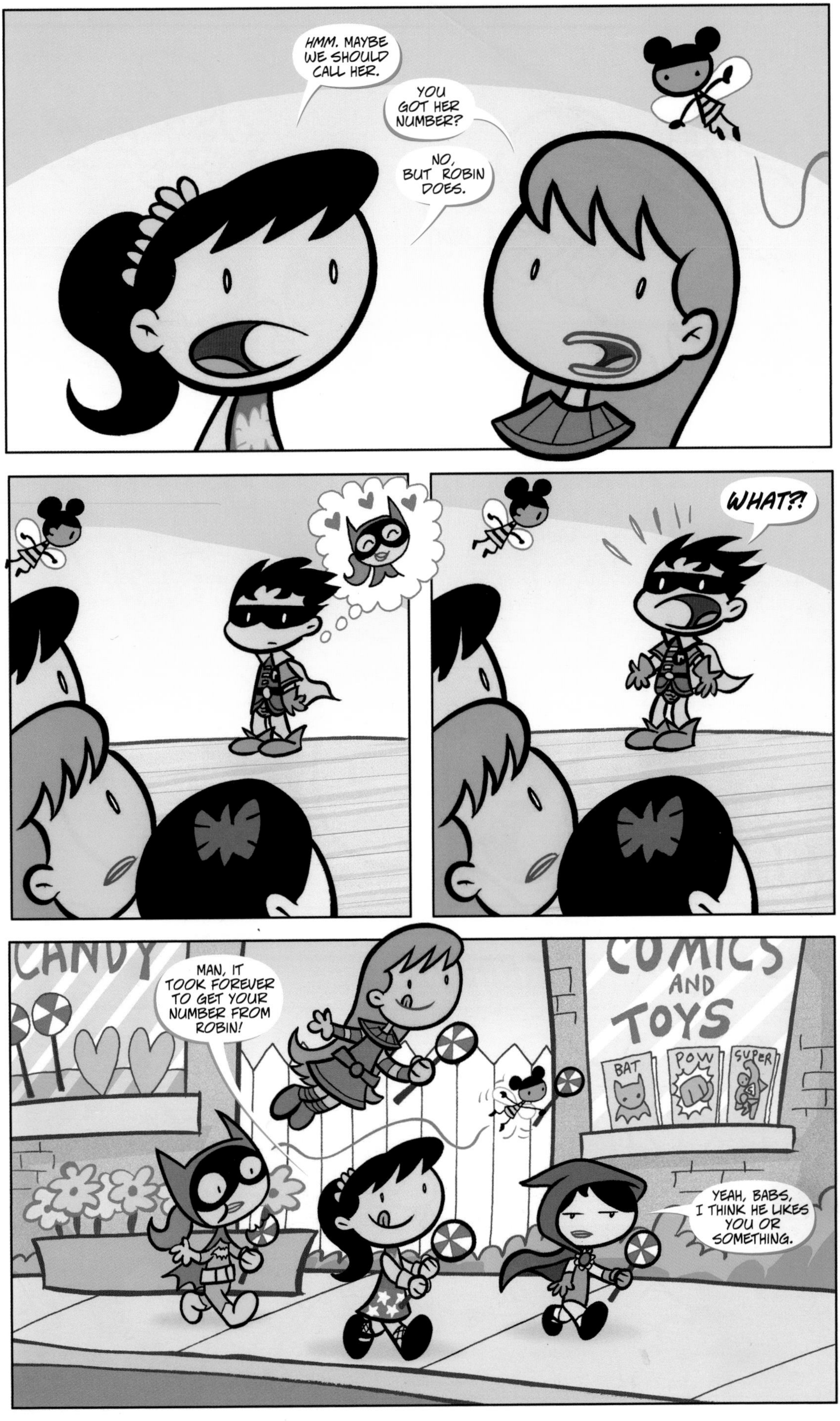
HMM. MAYBE WE SHOULD CALL HER.
YOU GOT HER NUMBER?
NO, BUT ROBIN DOES.
WHAT?!
CANDY
MAN, IT TOOK FOREVER TO GET YOUR NUMBER FROM ROBIN!
COMICS AND TOYS
BAT
POW
SUPER
YEAH, BABS, I THINK HE LIKES YOU OR SOMETHING.

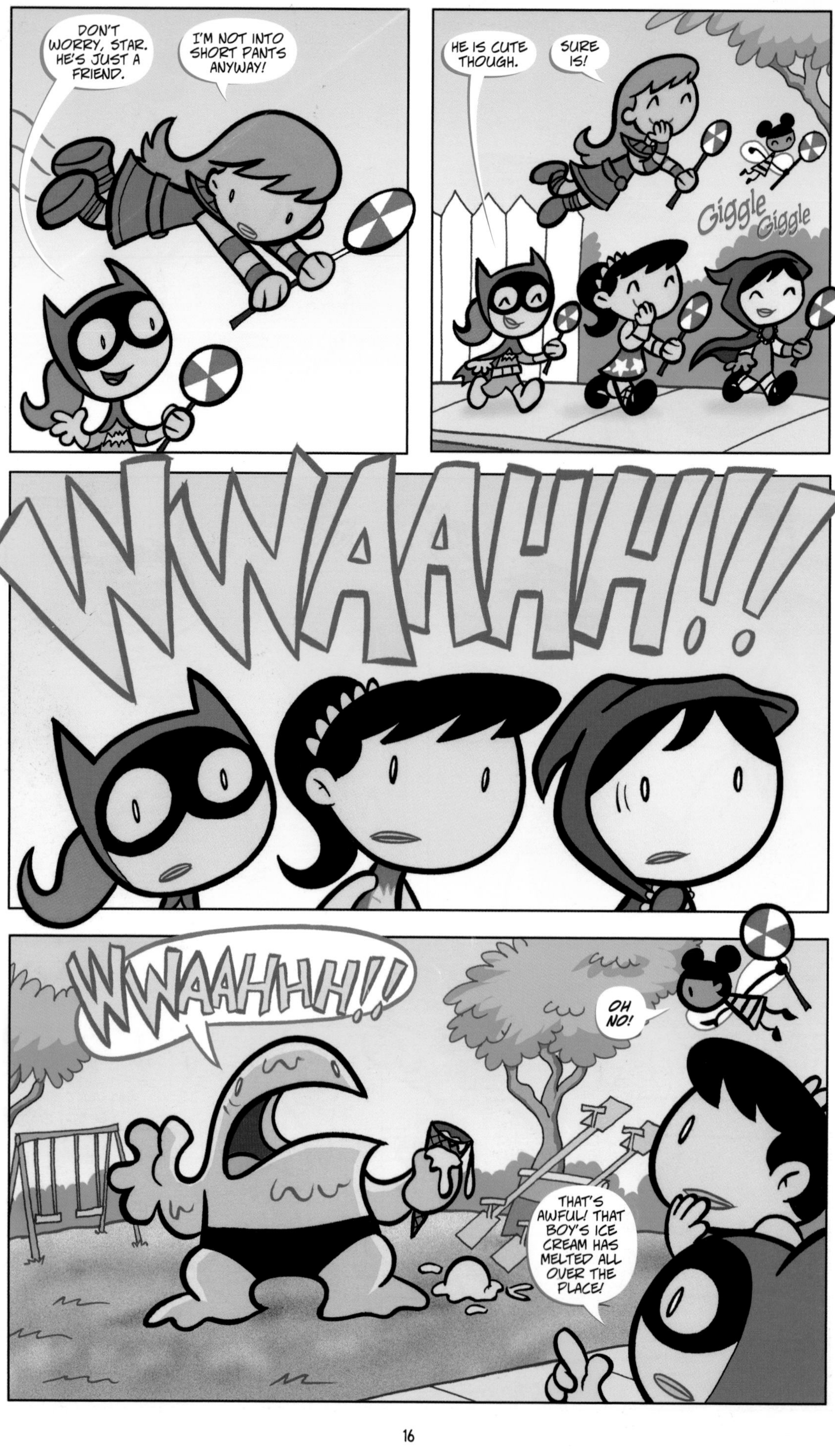
DON'T WORRY, STAR. HE'S JUST A FRIEND.
I'M NOT INTO SHORT PANTS ANYWAY!
HE IS CUTE THOUGH.
SURE IS!
Giggle Giggle
WWAAHH!!
WWAAHHH!!
OH NO!
THAT'S AWFUL! THAT BOY'S ICE CREAM HAS MELTED ALL OVER THE PLACE!

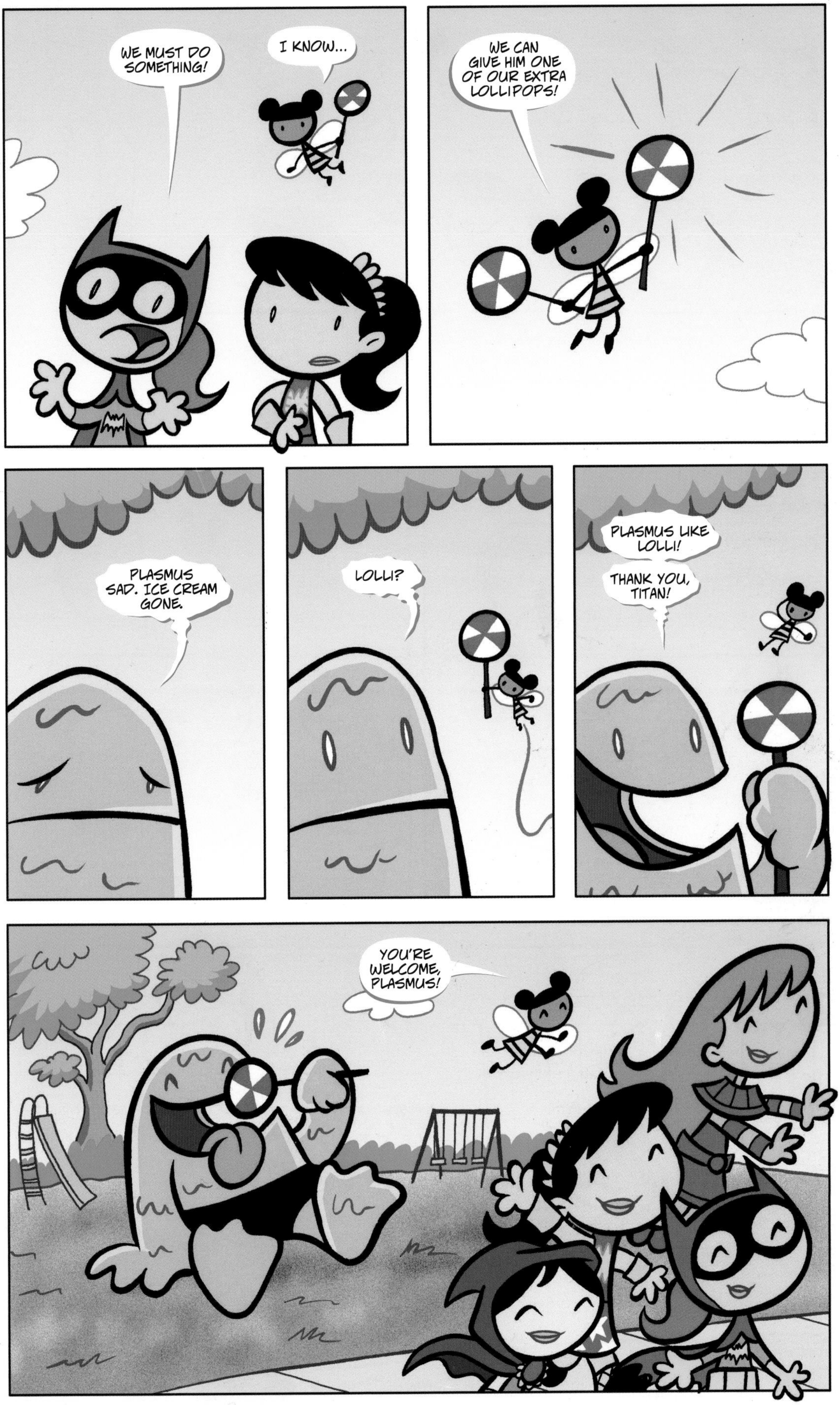
WE MUST DO SOMETHING!
I KNOW...
WE CAN GIVE HIM ONE OF OUR EXTRA LOLLIPOPS!
PLASMUS SAD. ICE CREAM GONE.
LOLLI?
PLASMUS LIKE LOLLI!
THANK YOU, TITAN!
YOU'RE WELCOME, PLASMUS!

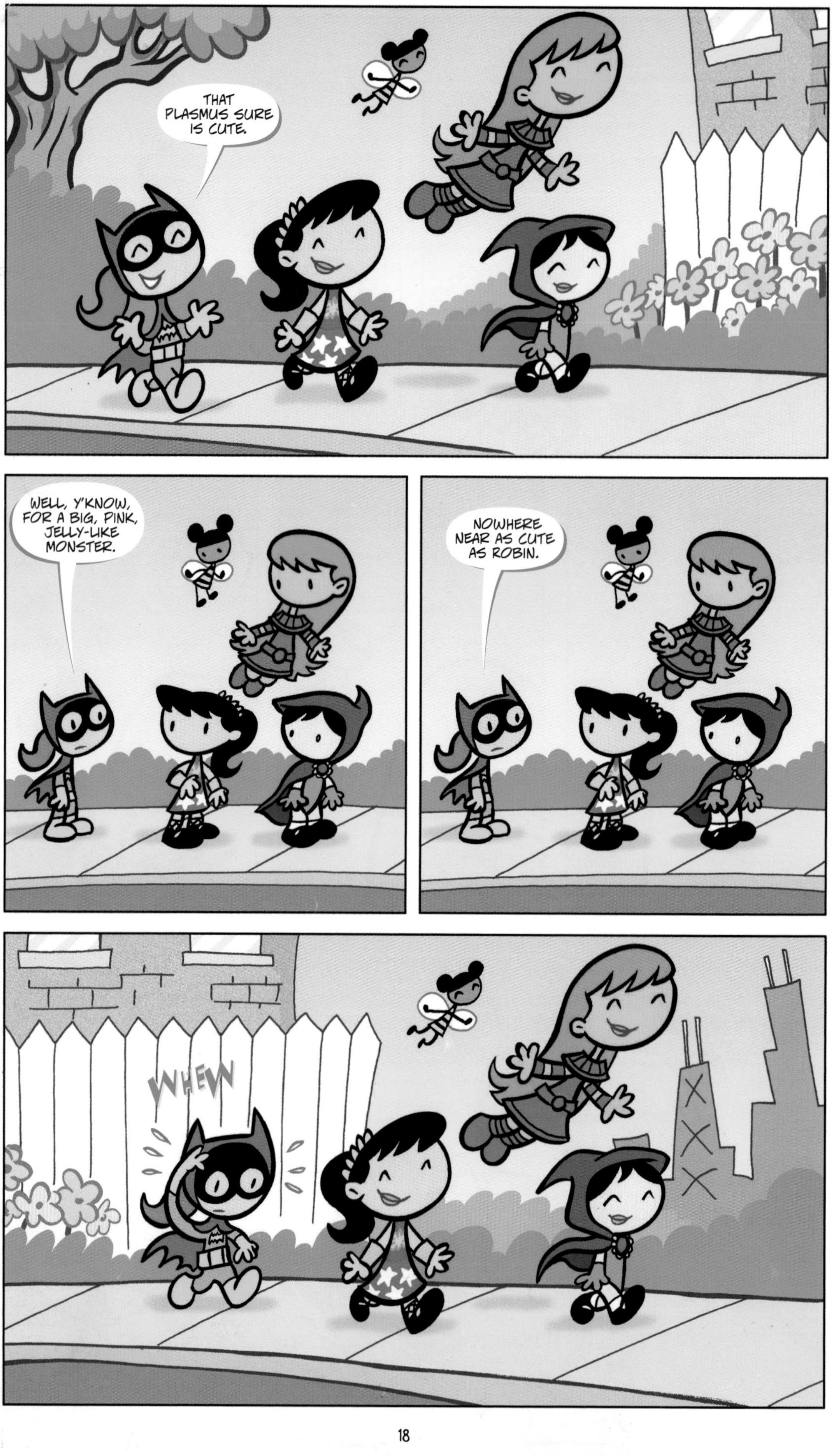
THAT PLASMUS SURE IS CUTE.
WELL, Y'KNOW, FOR A BIG, PINK, JELLY-LIKE MONSTER.
NOWHERE NEAR AS CUTE AS ROBIN.
WHEW

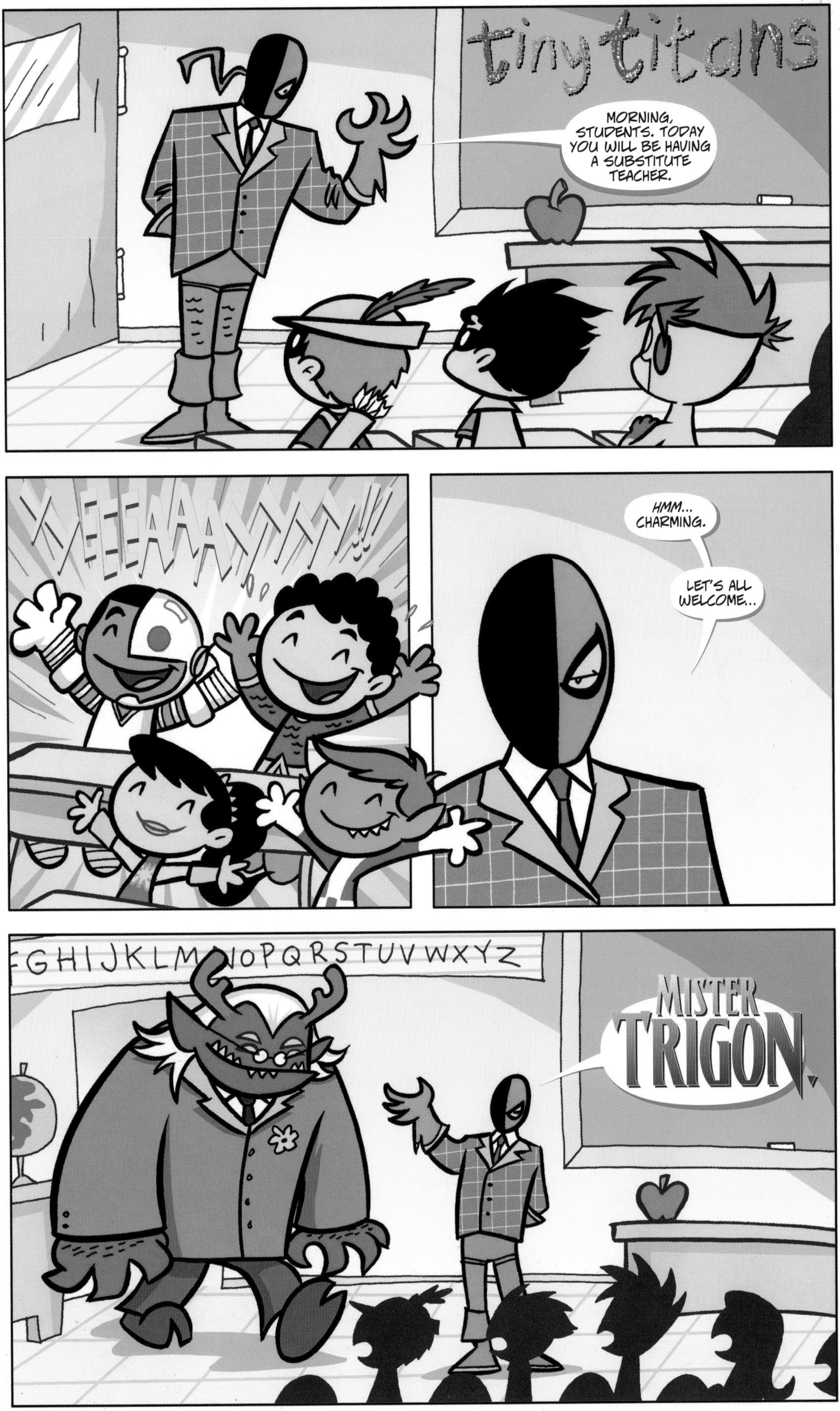
tiny titans
MORNING, STUDENTS. TODAY YOU WILL BE HAVING A SUBSTITUTE TEACHER.
YYEEEAAAYYYY!!!
HMM... CHARMING.
LET'S ALL WELCOME...
EFGHIJKLMNOPQRSTUVWXYZ
MISTER TRIGON.

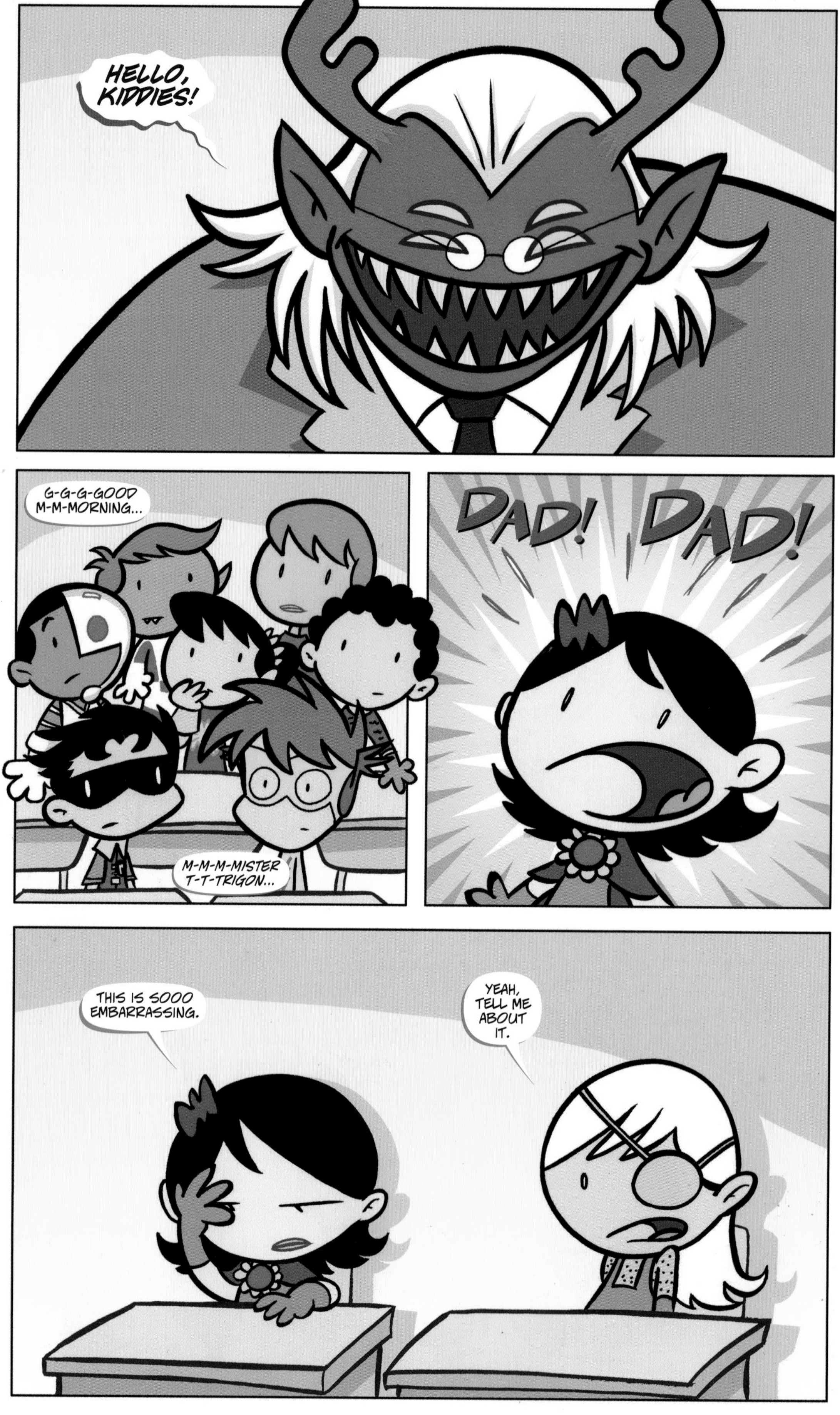

HELLO, KIDDIES!
G-G-G-GOOD M-M-MORNING...
M-M-M-MISTER T-T-TRIGON...
DAD! DAD!
THIS IS SOOO EMBARRASSING.
YEAH, TELL ME ABOUT IT.

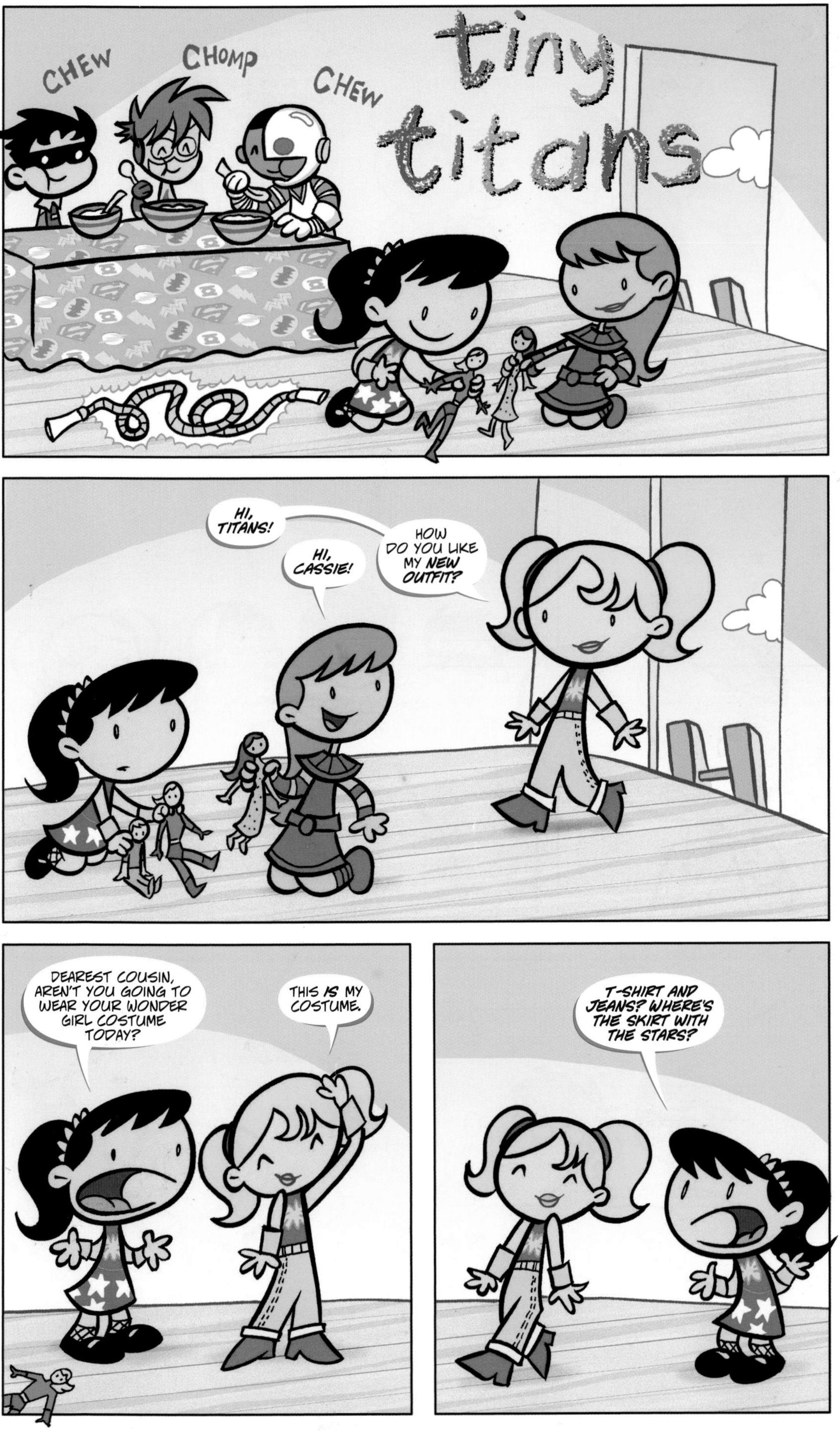
CHEW
CHOMP
CHEW
tiny titans
HI, TITANS!
HI, CASSIE!
HOW DO YOU LIKE MY NEW OUTFIT?
DEAREST COUSIN, AREN'T YOU GOING TO WEAR YOUR WONDER GIRL COSTUME TODAY?
THIS IS MY COSTUME.
T-SHIRT AND JEANS? WHERE'S THE SKIRT WITH THE STARS?

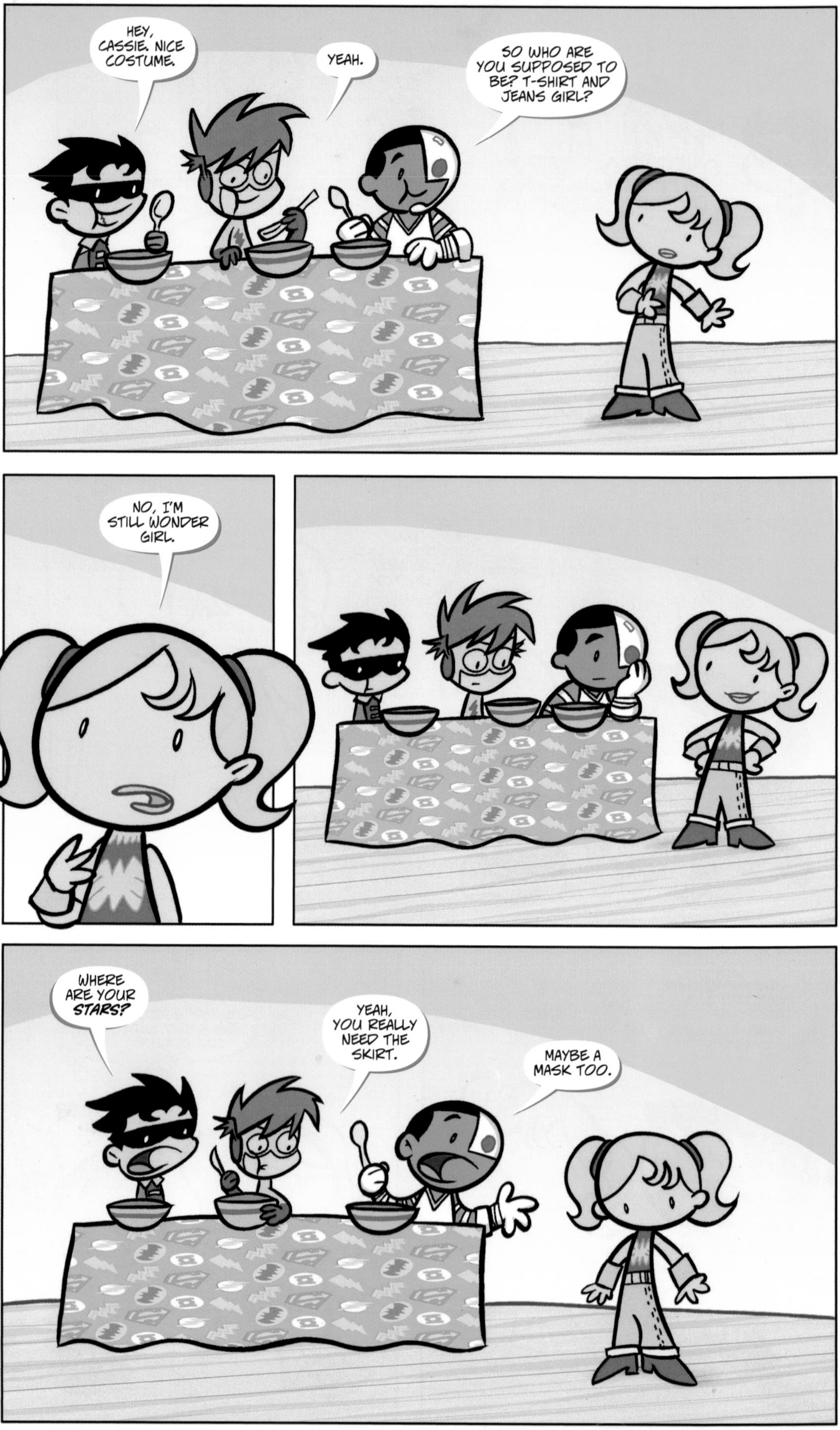
HEY, CASSIE. NICE COSTUME.
YEAH.
SO WHO ARE YOU SUPPOSED TO BE? T-SHIRT AND JEANS GIRL?
NO, I'M STILL WONDER GIRL.
WHERE ARE YOUR STARS?
YEAH, YOU REALLY NEED THE SKIRT.
MAYBE A MASK TOO.

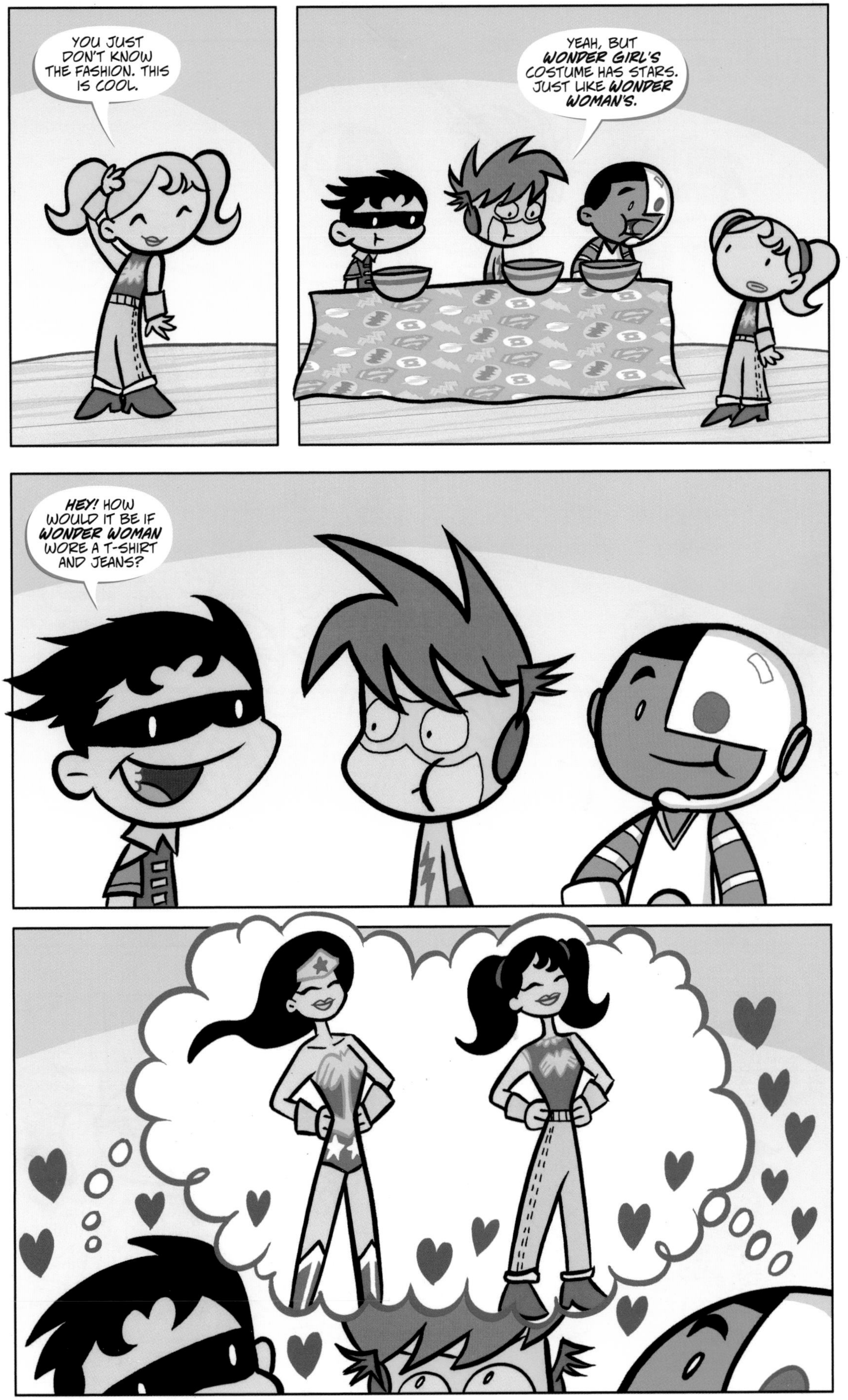
YOU JUST DON'T KNOW THE FASHION. THIS IS COOL.
YEAH, BUT WONDER GIRL'S COSTUME HAS STARS. JUST LIKE WONDER WOMAN'S.
HEY! HOW WOULD IT BE IF WONDER WOMAN WORE A T-SHIRT AND JEANS?

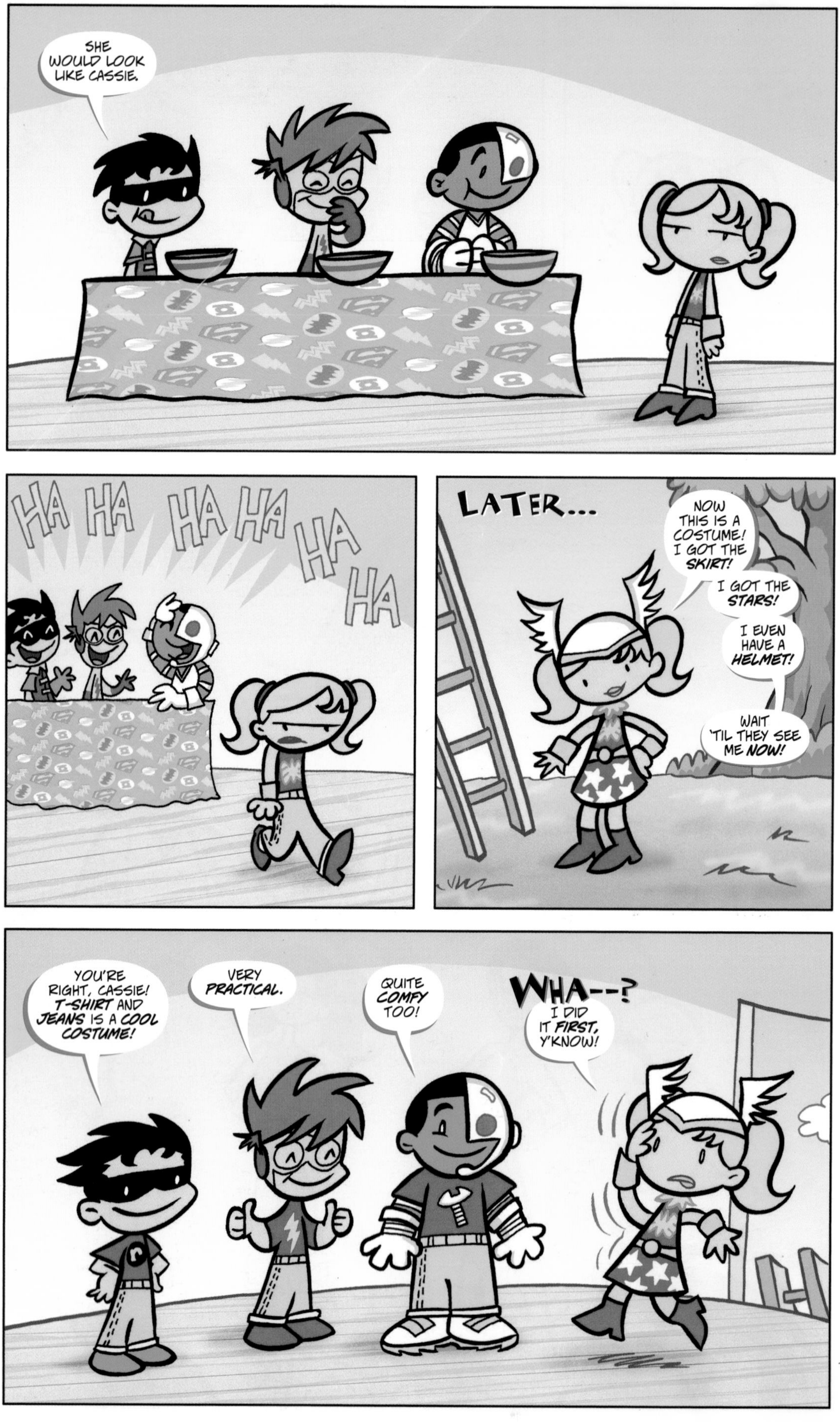

SHE WOULD LOOK LIKE CASSIE.
HA HA HA HA HA HA
LATER...
NOW THIS IS A COSTUME! I GOT THE SKIRT!
I GOT THE STARS!
I EVEN HAVE A HELMET!
WAIT 'TIL THEY SEE ME NOW!
YOU'RE RIGHT, CASSIE! T-SHIRT AND JEANS IS A COOL COSTUME!
VERY PRACTICAL.
QUITE COMFY TOO!
WHA--?
I DID IT FIRST, Y'KNOW!

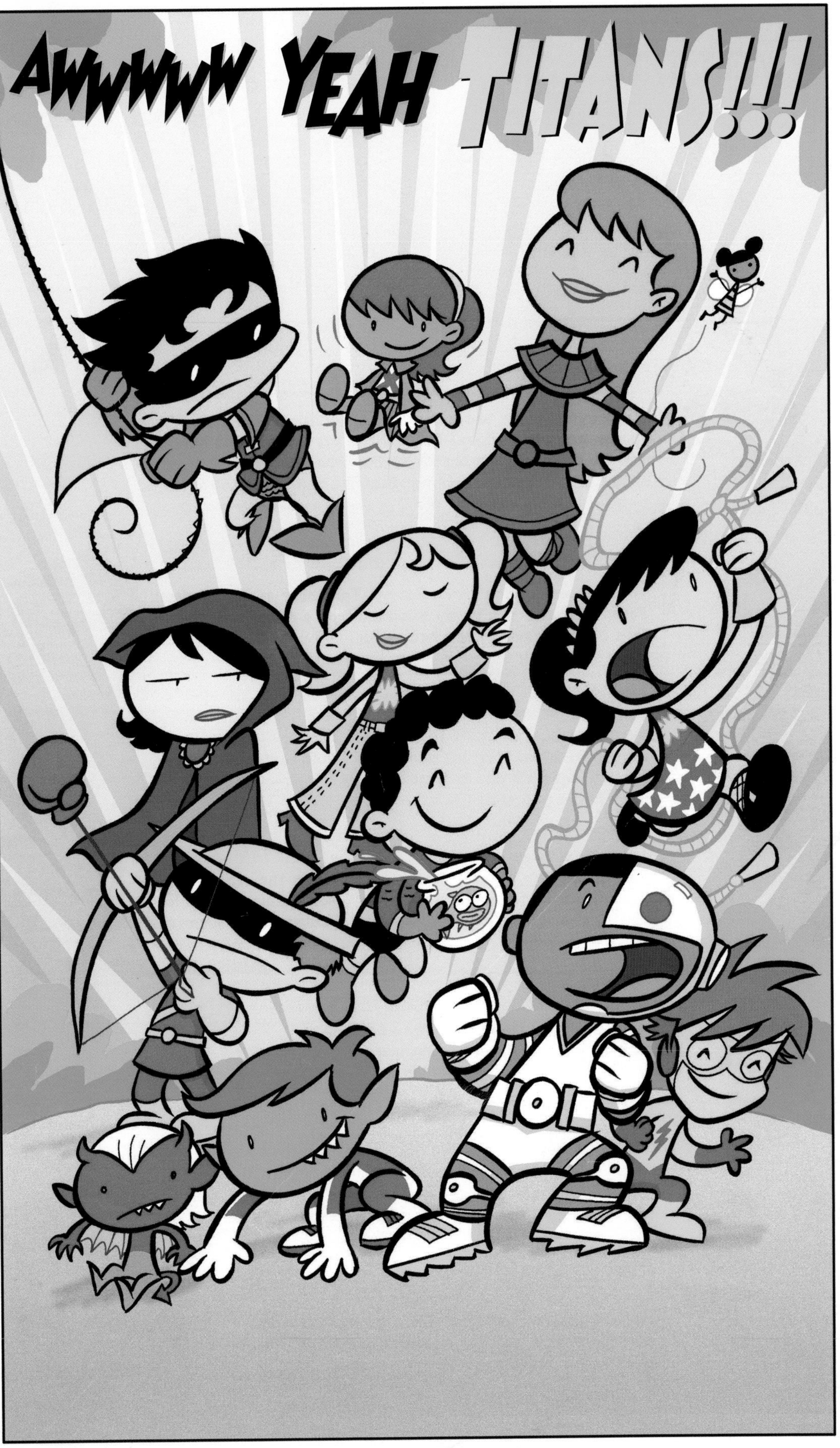
AWWWWW YEAH TITANS!!!
!
!

MEET THE... tiny titans

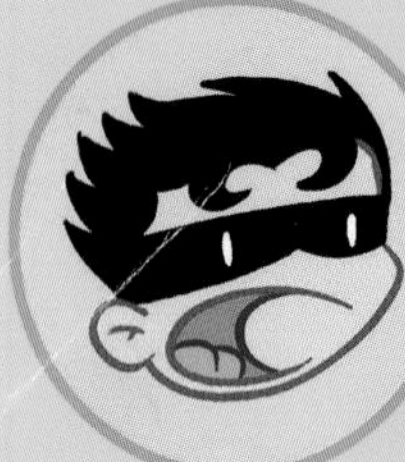

ROBIN

(Dick Grayson)- The brave and serious leader of the Tiny Titans. Although he is the original Robin, he is very moody and has to share his room with his brothers, the other Robins. Also, he has secret crushes for Starfire and Barbara Gordon.

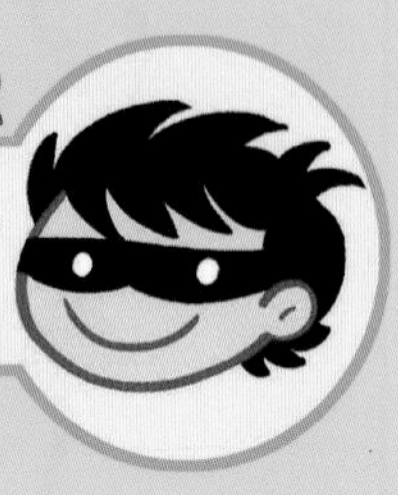

JASON TODDLER

The youngest of the three Robins. Too young to go to school, Jason is always in a happy mood and has a care-free style. He's all about smiling and having fun.

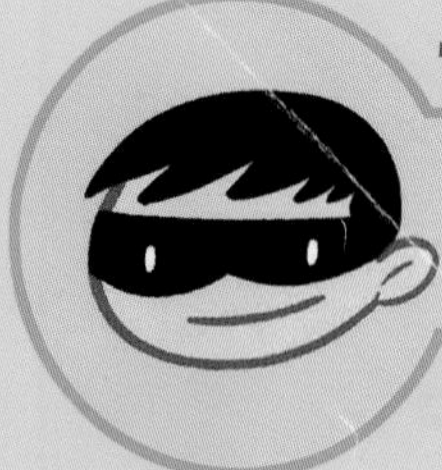

TIM DRAKE

The cool Robin. Tim wants to stand out from his brothers by wearing his own unique Robin costume. He's very laid back and easy going indeed.

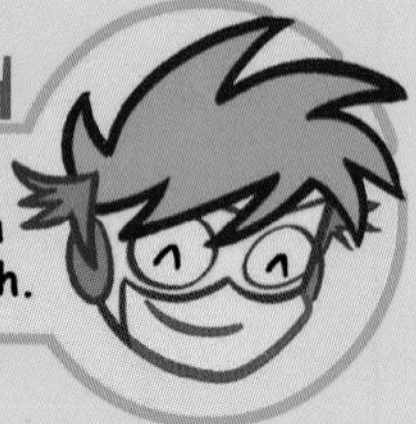

KID FLASH

The super speedster and fasted kid in the school. Quick witted and eats lots for lunch because of his high metabolism. Too much candy will cause major sugar rush.

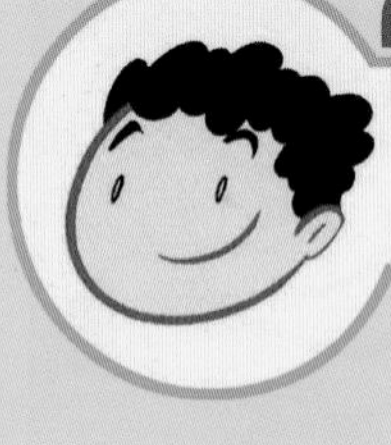

AQUALAD

The little boy from the ocean. Has a pet fish named Fluffy. Aqualad can communicate with all forms of sea life, even the pet hamster in their classroom.

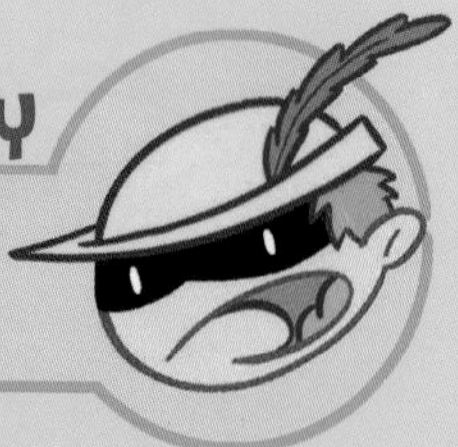

SPEEDY

Quiet and cool, he is the boy with the trick arrows. He's good at anything that requires aiming. Also, he's Kid Flash's best friend.

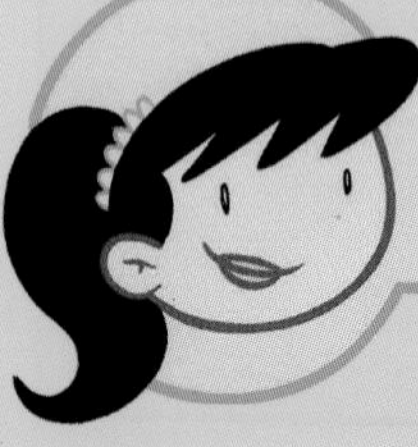

WONDER GIRL

(Donna) Raised by amazons. She's strong and cute. Never lie to her, she has a magical jump rope which makes people tell the truth. Very skeptic.

RAVEN

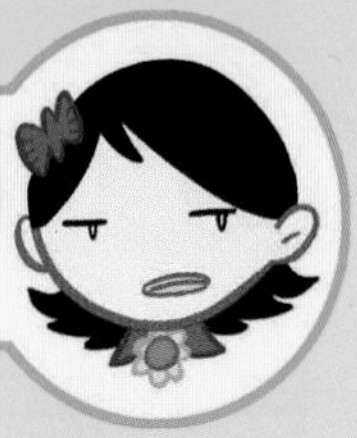

The quiet and mysterious little girl. She really likes to experiment with dark magic, which usually turn into bad practical jokes. Mr. Trigon, the substitute teacher is her father.

CYBORG

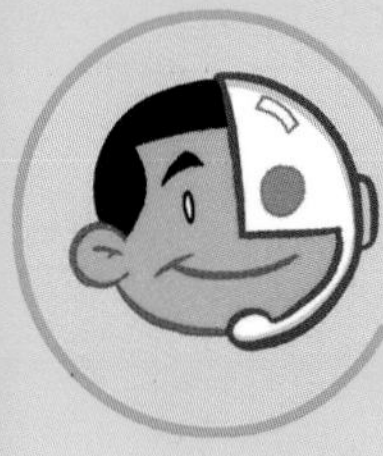

Half boy, half robot. Cyborg is always tinkering with mechanical gadgets, often turning them into something else. His battle cry "BOO-YA!" has earned him the nickname, "Big Boo-Ya".

BEAST BOY

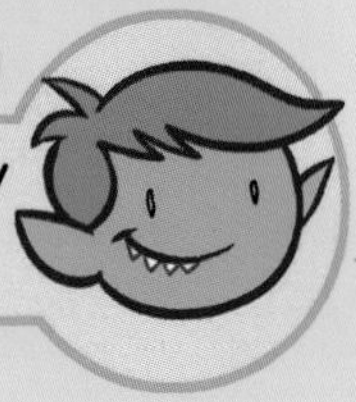

The green little boy who can change into any animal he desires. He's a prankster and loves comics. Has a crush on Terra.

STARFIRE

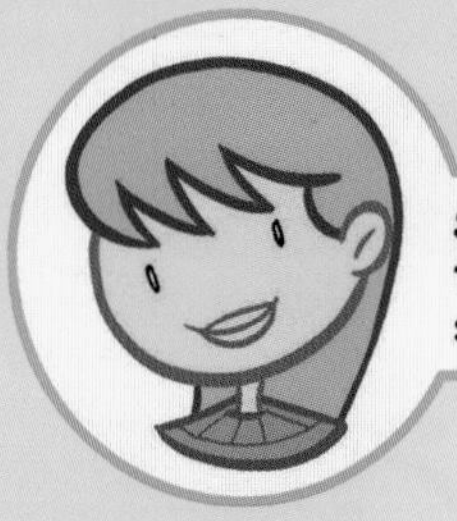

She's an alien princess. Very naïve and free spirited and finds the good in others. Has a crush on Robin and thinks he's cute, but so do all the other girls.

KID DEVIL

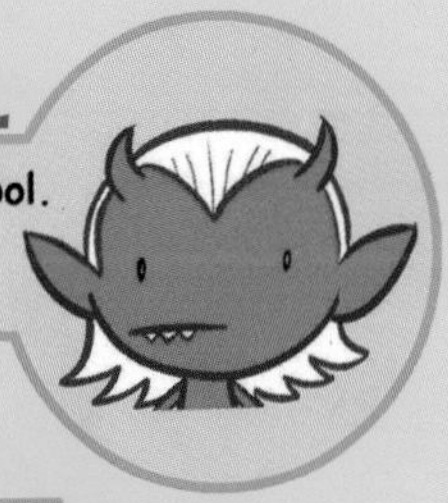

One of the younger Tiny Titans, still too young for school. Cannot talk but can breathe fire, usually while coughing or sneezing or hiccupping.

ROSE & JERICHO

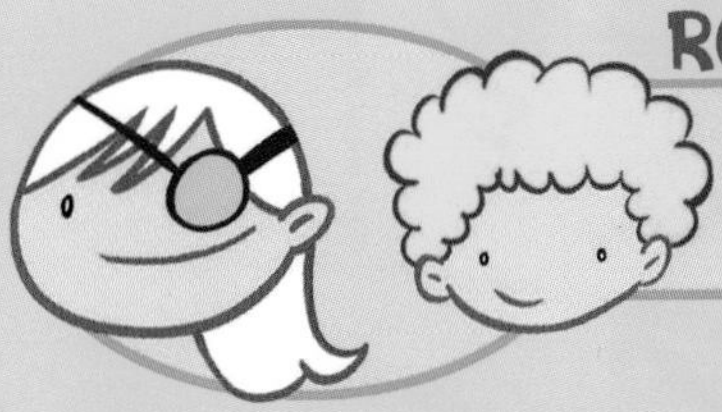

Principal Slade's kids. Rose is the older and tougher "Tom-Boy" of the two. Jericho can't speak, but can take over your mind if you look into his eyes.

MISS MARTIAN

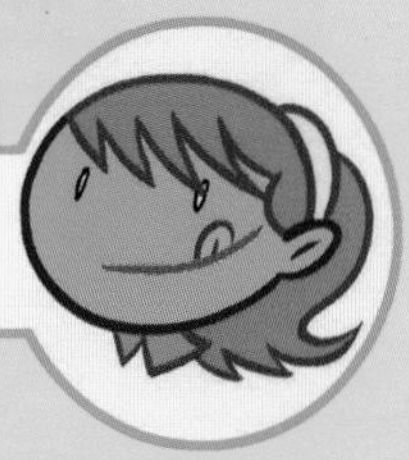

A shape shifting little girl alien from Mars who is still too young to go to school. She is often mistaken for Beast Boy's little sister.

TERRA

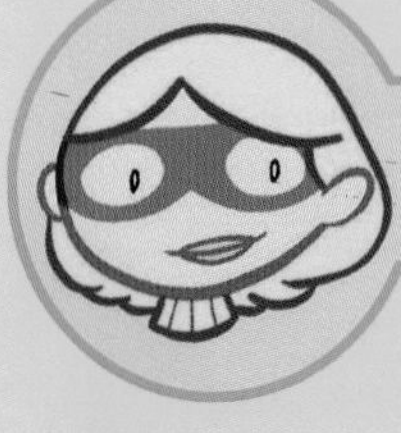

The sometimes hated little girl who likes to throw rocks. Principal Slade's teacher's pet. She thinks Beast Boy is a weirdo.

CASSIE

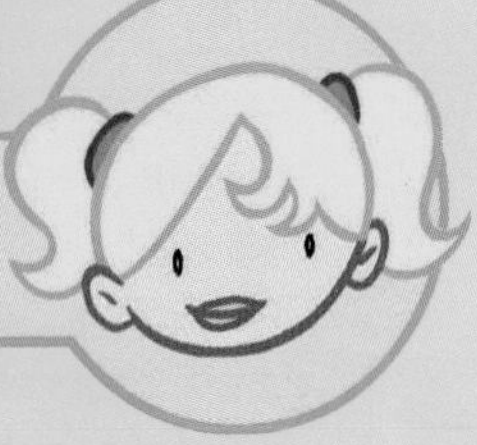

Wonder Girl's rich cousin from the big city. Cassie's really into fashion and is hip to all the latest trends in POP culture.

BUMBLE BEE

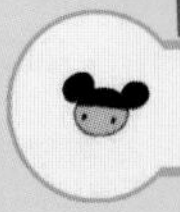

The tiniest of the Tiny Titans. BB buzzes and packs a mighty stinger.

Creators

Art Baltazar is a cartoonist machine from the heart of Chicago! He defines cartoons and comics not only as an art style, but as a way of life. Currently, Art is the creative force behind *The New York Times* best-selling, Eisner Award-winning, DC Comics series Tiny Titans, and the co-writer for Billy Batson and the Magic of SHAZAM! and co-creator of Superman Family Adventures. Art is living the dream! He draws comics and never has to leave the house. He lives with his lovely wife, Rose, big boy Sonny, little boy Gordon, and little girl Audrey. Right on!

ART BALTAZAR

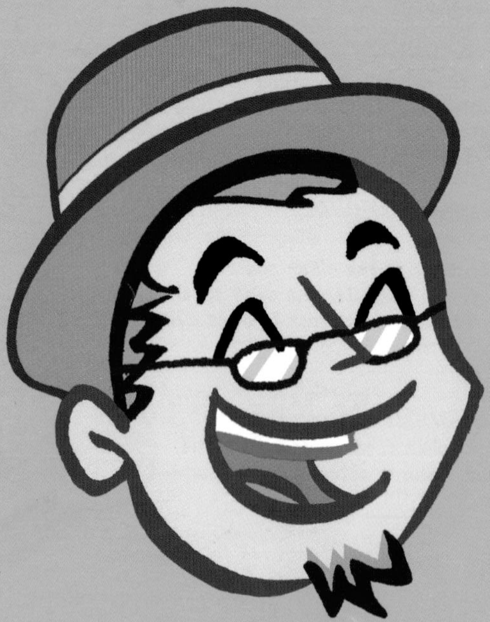

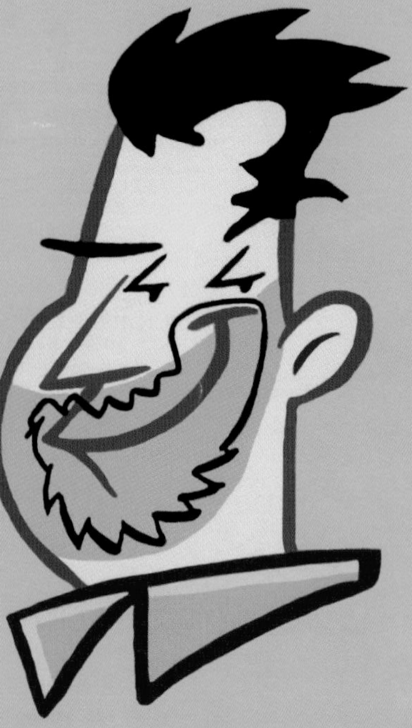

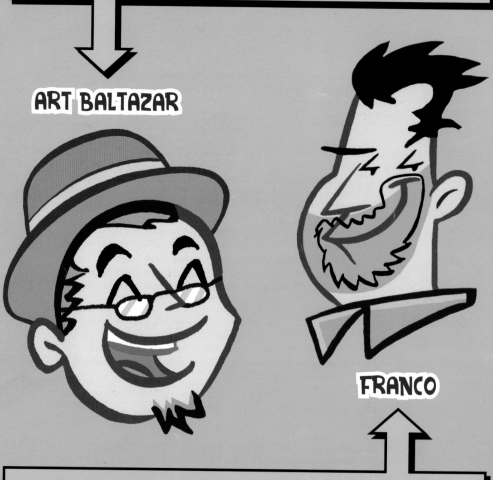

FRANCO

Bronx, New York born writer and artist Franco Aureliani has been drawing comics since he could hold a crayon. Currently residing in upstate New York with his wife, Ivette, and son, Nicolas, Franco spends most of his days in a Batcave-like studio where he produces DC's Tiny Titans comics. In 1995, Franco founded Blindwolf Studios, an independent art studio where he and fellow creators can create children's comics. Franco is the creator, artist, and writer of Weirdsville, L'il Creeps, and Eagle All Star, as well as the co-creator and writer of Patrick the Wolf Boy. When he's not writing and drawing, Franco also teaches high school art.

Glossary

COSTUME [KOSS·toom] - clothes worn by people or actors dressing in disguise

EMBARRASSING [em·BA·ruhss·ing] - something that makes you feel awkward or uncomfortable

PRACTICAL [PRAK·tuh·kuhl] - useful or sensible

PRINCIPAL [PRIN·suh·puhl] - the head of a public school

STRICT [STRIKT] - if someone is strict, the person makes you obey rules exactly and behave properly

SUBSTITUTE [SUHB·stuh·toot] - something or someone used in place of another

Action Accessories

Speedy

BOW AND ARROW

Robin

CAPE

Terra

ROCKS

Aqualad

FLUFFY

Wonder Girl

MAGIC JUMP ROPE

Visual Questions & Prompts

1. IN COMICS, THE WAY A CHARACTER'S EYES AND MOUTH LOOK CAN SHOW HOW HE OR SHE IS FEELING. BELOW, HOW DO YOU THINK PLASMUS IS FEELING IN EACH OF THE THREE PANELS? USE THE ILLUSTRATION TO EXPLAIN YOUR ANSWER.

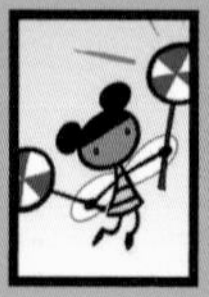

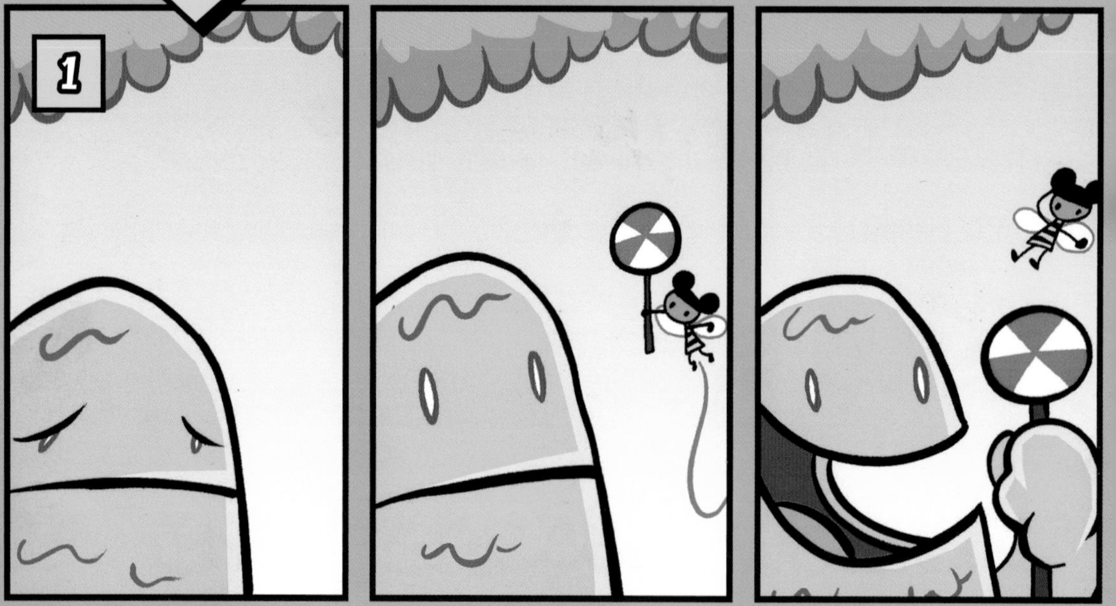
1

2. THE TINY TITANS ARE EXCITED WHEN THEY HEAR THEY'LL HAVE A SUBSTITUTE TEACHER. WHEN YOU SAW THE SUBSTITUTE TEACHER, DID YOU THINK HE WAS NICE OR MEAN? WHY?

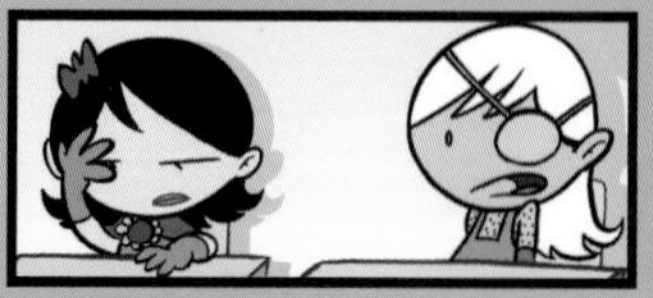

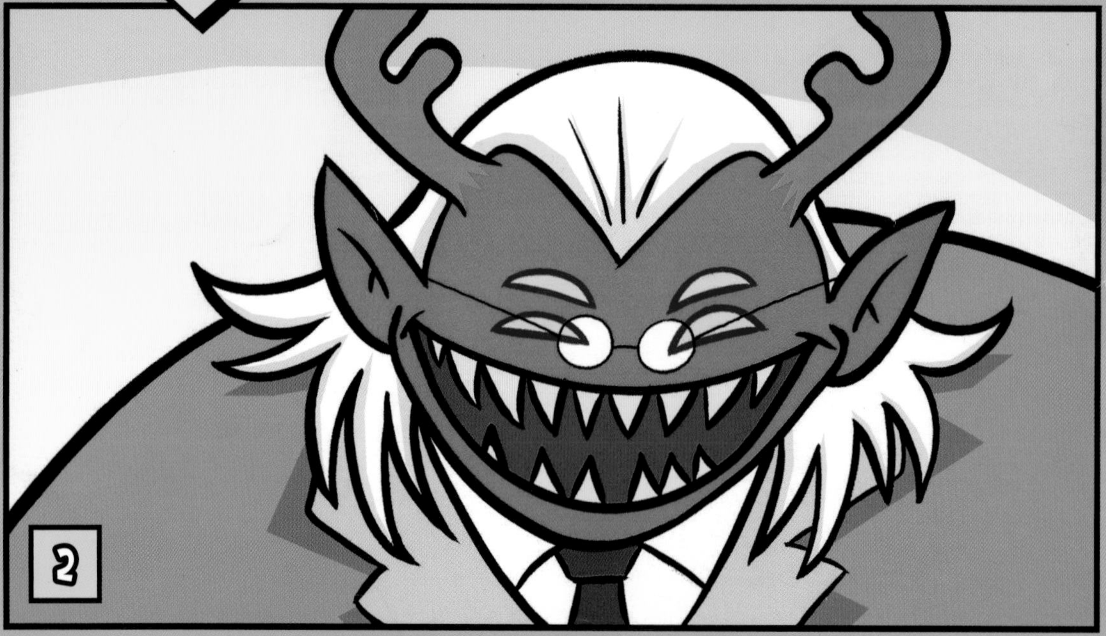
2

3. WHEN ROSE FINDS OUT THAT HER DAD IS THE PRINCIPAL, SHE FEELS EMBARRASSED. HOW CAN YOU TELL FROM THE PANEL AT RIGHT THAT ROSE IS EMBARRASSED?

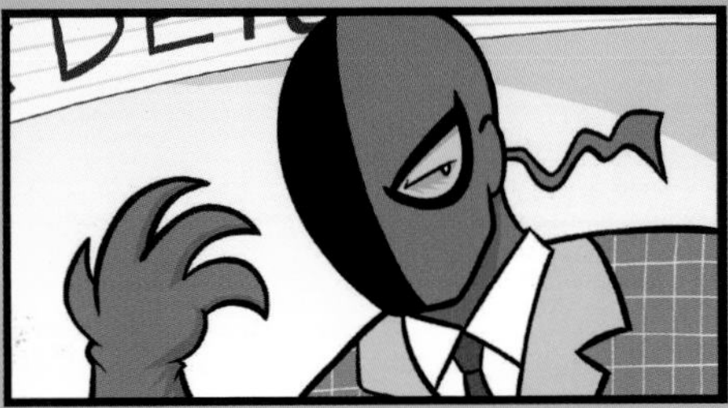

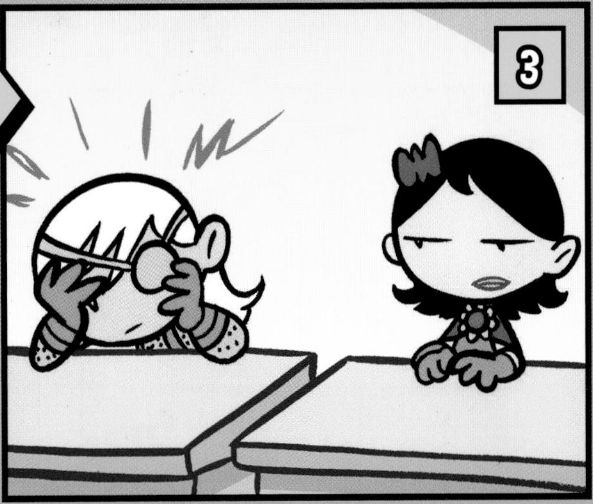
3

4. SOMETIMES YOU DON'T NEED WORDS IN ORDER TO TELL A STORY. WRITE 2-3 SENTENCES EXPLAINING THE STORY IN THE PANELS BELOW.

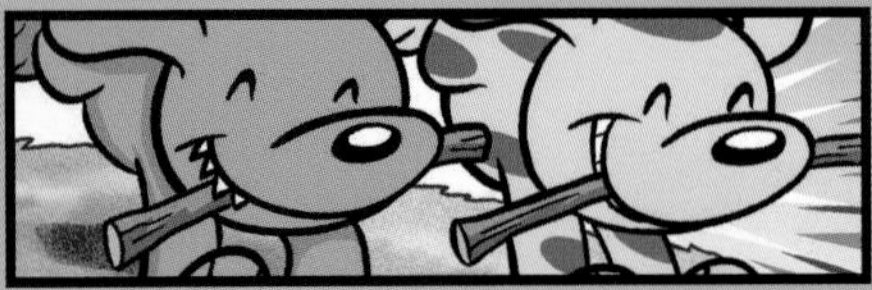

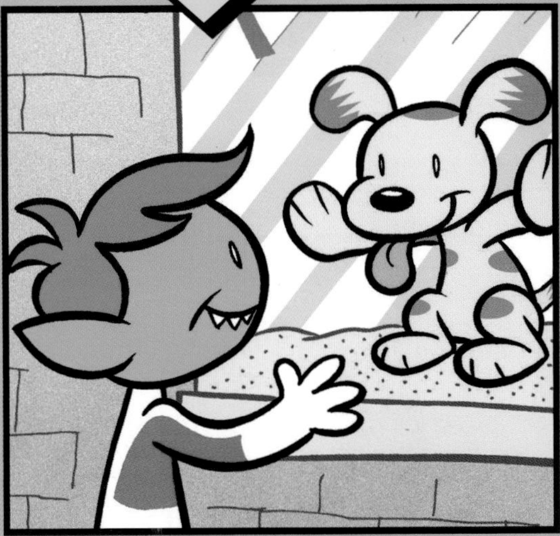

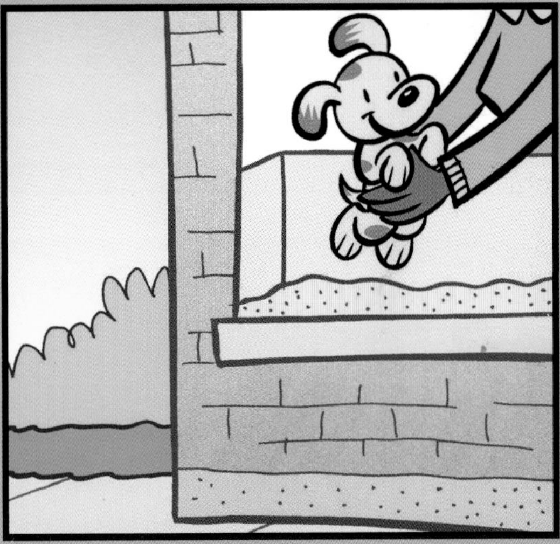

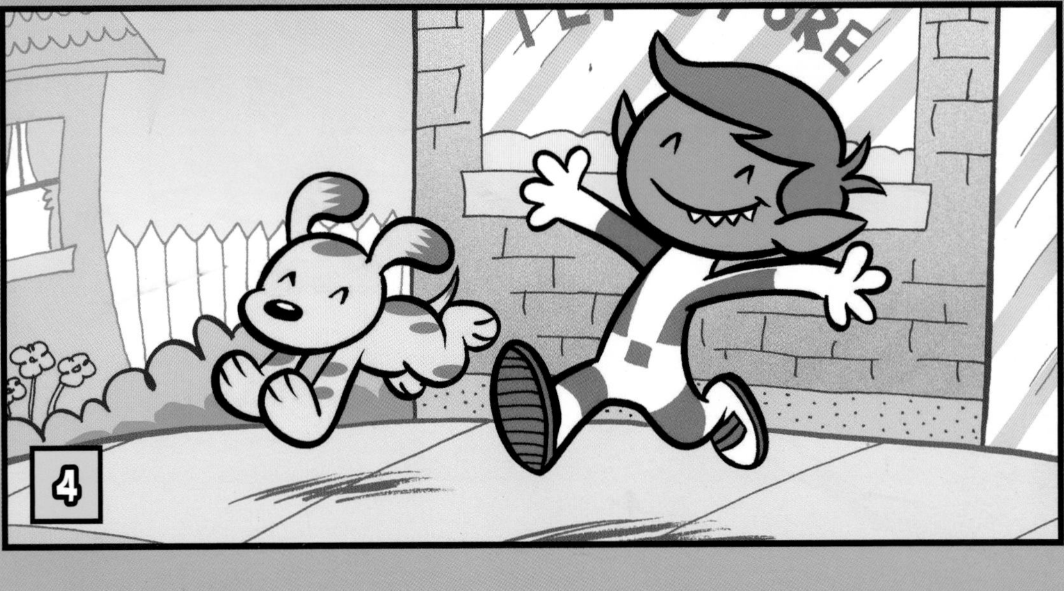
4

tiny titans

FIND COOL WEBSITES AND MORE BOOKS LIKE THIS ONE AT WWW.FACTHOUND.COM.

JUST TYPE IN THE BOOK ID: 9781434245281

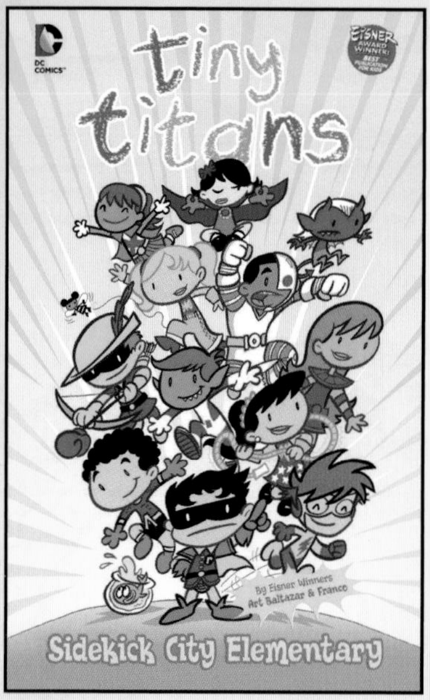
DC COMICS
EISNER AWARD WINNER!
tiny titans
By Eisner Winners Art Baltazar & Franco
Sidekick City Elementary

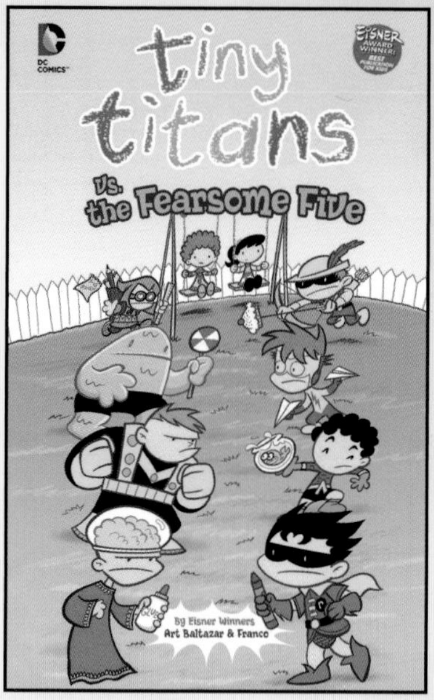
DC COMICS
EISNER AWARD WINNER!
tiny titans
vs. the Fearsome Five
By Eisner Winners Art Baltazar & Franco

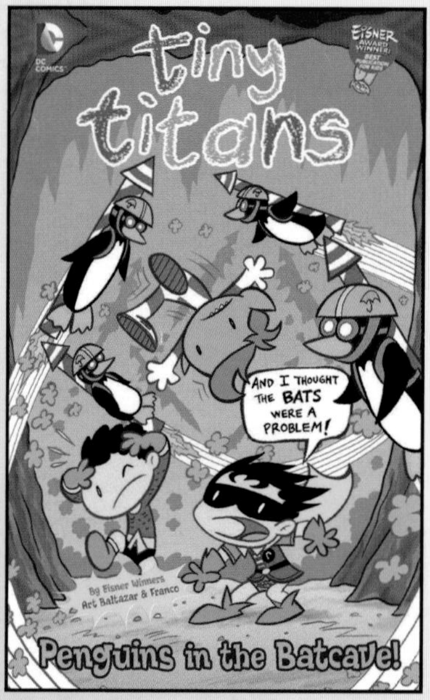
DC COMICS
EISNER AWARD WINNER!
tiny titans
AND I THOUGHT THE BATS WERE A PROBLEM!
By Eisner Winners Art Baltazar & Franco
Penguins in the Batcave!

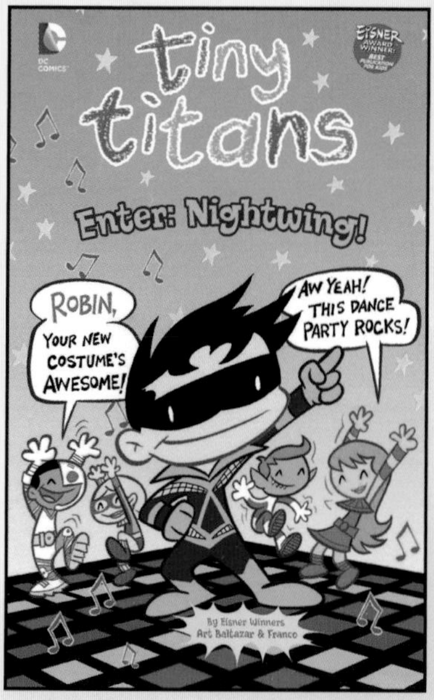
DC COMICS
EISNER AWARD WINNER!
tiny titans
Enter: Nightwing!
ROBIN, YOUR NEW COSTUME'S AWESOME!
AW YEAH! THIS DANCE PARTY ROCKS!
By Eisner Winners Art Baltazar & Franco

WANT EVEN MORE COMICS?

TO FIND A COMICS SHOP NEAR YOU:

CALL 1-888 COMIC BOOK

OR VISIT WWW.COMICSHOPLOCATOR.COM